A MACKENZIE FAMILY CHRISTMAS

THE PERFECT GIFT

JENNIFER ASHLEY

Mackenzie Family Christmas: The Perfect Gift

Mackenzies Book 4.5

Cover design by Kim Killion

CHAPTER ONE

December 1884

Ian Mackenzie hated funerals.

He especially hated dour, overly long funerals that dragged family and friends out to the side of a damp grave in the middle of a Scottish December, wind coming off the hills to chill the bone.

The only warmth was Beth, standing at his side like a bright flame. She wore a dark gray frock trimmed with black, in keeping with the solemn occasion, but she could have been dressed in fiery red for the heat that suffused Ian. Because of Beth, he was able to come today and pay his respects to an old neighbor.

The minister droned on about man being cut down like a flower in his prime—ridiculous, because Mrs. McCray had been ninety. A Sassenach from northern England, she'd married the laird in the next valley, a crony of Ian's father. Now Mrs. McCray and her husband were gone, and her sons, tall Scots lads who'd already produced more tall Scots lads, would take over the lands.

The funeral ended, somber to the last. The McCrays had been very stern, very Scots, very Protestant, Mrs. McCray just as stern as her husband. Decadence strictly forbidden. And the Mackenzies, her neighbors, were so very decadent.

"'Twill be quieter around these parts without her, that's certain," Mac Mackenzie said as they walked back home, Beth close to Ian, Mac arm in arm with his wife Isabella.

Hart was riding back in his carriage, the Duke of Kilmorgan ever aware of his dignity. He'd come alone, as Eleanor, his new bride, was too far gone with their first child to make the journey to the chill funeral.

"She never spoke except in a voice that would shatter glass," Mac went on. He put on a falsetto. *"Roland Mackenzie, when are you going to leave off painting that trash and settle yourself like a gentleman? You disgrace yourself, your family, and your father. I can still hear her, poor woman."*

"Surely she left off after your marriage turned happy," Beth said behind him. "And you produced a son and heir."

"No," Mac said, turning to flash his wide grin. "That was last week."

"She went swiftly, which was a mercy," Isabella said. Wind stirred the dark blue feathers in her hat, and Mac's reddish hair. "She was working in her garden. Never felt a thing."

"That's how I want to go," Mac said. "Walking upright one moment, flat on my nose the next."

Isabella moved a step closer to him. "Let us not speak of it."

"Aye," Cameron Mackenzie said. A sharp gust billowed back his long black coat, and shoved his hair from his sharp face. "Too many bloody funerals in this family already."

Ainsley slid an arm around his waist. Cameron, the largest Mackenzie, bent his head as he pulled his wife to him.

Ian felt Beth close on him as well, her gloved hands on his arm. All thoughts of funerals, old Mrs. McCray, and cold Scots winters dissolved. Ian had Beth, and nothing else mattered.

They walked down the hill to the valley that held Kilmorgan Castle. Kilmorgan Castle was a large manor house, the old castle having been destroyed a hundred and more years ago in the Jacobite rebellion. Malcolm Mackenzie, who'd survived the Battle of Culloden Moor had raised a gigantic Georgian structure in its place.

Ian, as always, felt lighter as he beheld the beautiful symmetry of the house—four wings of identical dimensions running back from a long perpendicular wing. The long wing was proportional to the four shorter wings by exactly two to one, not an inch out of place. The height of the house likewise was pleasingly proportional to its breadth and depth. Ian had studied the house meticulously over the years, measuring it to the last fraction. His father had tried to beat the obsession out of him, but Ian had taken comfort in the precise calculations.

Behind the house, formal gardens had been laid out in the same kind of mirrored symmetry. Mac said he found the entire setup stifling, but the astonishing simplicity of the house and gardens had helped keep the young Ian from complete despair.

Now he shared this beauty with Beth . . . he shared so many things with her.

The house's massive front hall welcomed them with warmth, made still more cheerful by the greenery and ribbons the ladies of the house had hung here, there, and everywhere. *Like I'm walking through a bloody woods*, Hart had growled, but without any true rancor behind his words.

Curry, Ian's valet, met them in the hall and ushered the family into the private dining room, where warm tea, coffee, whiskey, wine, and plenty of food awaited them. Curry, a Cockney man who'd helped Ian through the worst days of the asylum, considered funerals bad luck, especially funerals of a lady who'd turned a rough tongue on Curry on more than one occasion, and so had stayed home.

Hart, having arrived before them, insisted they lift at least one glass to old Mrs. McCray. "May she, her husband, and our father be bullying one another in the great beyond."

"I hope they enjoy it," Mac said, lifting his glass. His cut crystal goblet held tea, not whiskey. Mac now drank no alcohol of any kind.

"Confusion to them all," Cam said, joining the toast.

Hart downed his single malt in silence, then he left the room, off to seek Eleanor. The ladies sipped, each enjoying a warm spiced wine, but Ian didn't drink.

"She wasn't cruel," Ian said into the lull.

The others turned to him in surprise, as they often

did when Ian added to a conversation long after that conversation had ceased.

"No?" Mac asked, an edge of anger in his voice. "She urged Father to have you committed as a lunatic, and then told Hart he made a mistake letting you out of the asylum again."

"She thought she was helping me," Ian said. "Father wanted rid of me. There is a difference."

Mac studied him for a moment with an unreadable expression, then went back to the exotic tea his valet kept brewed for him. "If you say so, little brother."

"She were a right bother, that's for certain" Curry said, approaching with more whiskey. "Forgive me bluntness. But old Mrs. McCray could be kind too. She took in urchins, gave 'em a warm belly and a job."

"In return for a piece of her mind," Mac said.

"Aye, that's so. But when you're starving, you're not so choosy. As I know."

Ian sipped his whiskey and sat down with Beth, no longer interested. Mac laughed at Curry. "You mean, the Mackenzies took you in, and in return, you have to put up with us?"

"Now, I'd never say something like that, your lordship," Curry said. His eyes twinkled, and he tipped Beth a wink, but Ian had lost the flow of the conversation. The funeral, Mrs. McCray, and all that it meant, were finished.

"By the way," Curry said, coming to Ian with the decanter. "While you were out, it came."

Ian waited while Curry filled his glass, Ian taking in the flow of the amber liquid, the exact way the droplets splashed into the glass and spread in perfect ripples.

When Curry finished and took a step back, his words, along with Beth's excited smile, connected in Ian's brain.

"It's here?" Ian asked.

"Aye, m'lord. Waiting for you in the Ming room. With the Russian gentleman's compliments, his man who delivered it said."

Ian didn't hear the last. He left his seat, his brothers, their wives, and Curry a blur as he strode out of the room and down the enormous corridor, not realizing until halfway that he still clutched a full glass of whiskey, the liquid sloshing out over his hand.

BETH WALKED OUT AFTER IAN, HER SKIRTS RUSTLING, but she didn't hurry. She knew where her husband was going and why.

This summer, Ian had found an illustration of a Ming bowl in a book he'd read with his usual speed, and nothing would do but that he acquired said bowl, no matter what the cost.

He'd scoured antiques stores in London, Edinburgh, Paris, and down into Italy. He'd visited dealers, written letters, sent telegrams, and waited anxiously for the answers. Because Ian was one of the foremost collectors of Ming bowls in Great Britain and Europe, many came forward to say they had a bowl exactly like it, but Ian had always known that none of them were right. *It isn't the same,* he'd tell the disappointed merchant or collector.

At long last, he'd pinned down the current owner of the bowl in the book—an aristocrat in Russia. The

Russian gentleman had agreed to the price and said he'd send the bowl by courier. Impatient Ian had thought of little else from that day to this.

Beth found him at a table in the middle of the Ming room, his broad hands tearing back the paper and straw in a wooden box. She paused to observe him, her tall husband with a blue and green Mackenzie kilt hugging his hips, his dark formal coat stretched across his shoulders. He'd mussed his close-cropped hair, lamplight burnishing auburn streaks in it.

He worked quickly, gaze intent on the box. The room around him was filled floor to ceiling with glassed-in shelves and glass cases on the floor, each bearing a Ming bowl on a little stand, each precisely labeled.

Bowls only. Ian had no interest in vases or in porcelain from any other period. His early Ming collection, however, was priceless, the envy of all other Ming aficionados.

Ian lifted the bowl from the wrappings and swiftly examined it, holding it up to the light and studying every side. Beth held her breath, fearing the Russian had cheated him, and wondering what Ian's reaction would be if he had.

Then Ian relaxed into his devastating smile, his golden gaze seeking hers. "My Beth, come and see."

He held the bowl with steady fingers as he waited for her. Beth marveled that his hands, so large and strong, could be so gentle—with his Ming bowls, on her skin, while holding his son and daughter.

The bowl was certainly beautiful. Its thin porcelain sides were covered with interwoven flowers and tiny dragons in blue, one object flowing into another in delicate strokes. The inside of the bowl held more flowers dancing around the rim, and on the bottom was a single lotus flower. The underside held a dragon, four claws curled around the bowl's bottom lip. The blue, the only color, was incredible—dark and intense across the centuries.

"Lovely," Beth breathed. "I understand now why you hunted for it so hard."

Ian kept his gaze on the bowl, his face betraying joy he didn't know how to convey. He said nothing, but his look, his happiness, was enough.

"The perfect Christmas gift," Beth said. "How on earth will I find something for you to compete with it?"

"Today isn't Christmas," Ian said in his matter-of-fact voice, still looking at the bowl. "It's the twelfth. And we give our gifts at Hogmanay."

"No, I meant . . . Never mind." Ian could be so very literal, and though he did try to understand Beth's little jokes, he didn't always catch when she meant to be funny. *Poor Beth,* she imagined him thinking, *She doesn't understand a word she's saying.*

Ian set the bowl into her cupped palms. "Hold it up to the light. The pattern is deep. You can see the layers when th' light is behind them."

He kept hold of her wrists as he guided her to raise her hands, holding the bowl toward the warm yellow wall sconce, which dripped with long, clear crystals.

The light unfolded more flowers from between the dragons and vines, small and light blue. "Oh, Ian, it's exquisite."

Ian released her wrists to let her turn the bowl this way and that, but he remained behind her, his warmth on her back. Her bustle crushed against his legs, Ian's arm coming around her waist. He leaned to kiss her neck, the love in the kiss rippling heat through her.

Beth held the bowl up again, her fingers trembling. She needed to tell Ian of the outcome of their nights in bed this autumn, but she'd not had the chance yet. But now . . .

Beth started to turn, to lower the bowl, to hand it back to him.

Her shoe caught on the edge of the Aubusson carpet, its fringe snagging the high heel of her boot. She rocked, and Ian caught her by the elbow, but the bowl slipped from her fingers.

She lunged for it, and so did Ian, but the porcelain evaded their outstretched hands.

Beth watched in horror as the blue and white bowl fell down, down, down to the wooden floor beyond the rug, and smashed into shower of beautiful, polished bits.

CHAPTER TWO

*B*eth followed the bowl down, her dark skirts spreading as she sank to her knees. "Oh, Ian." Her breath caught on a sob. "Ian, I am so, so sorry."

Ian remained fixed beside her, his polished boots an inch from her skirts. His large hand curled against the blue and green plaid of his kilt, a silent sign of his anguish.

Beth reached for the pieces, tears in her eyes. What had she done? What had she *done*?

She found Ian on his knees next to her, his hands gently lifting hers from the broken shards. "You'll cut yourself."

His voice was even, almost a monotone. Ian's gaze fixed on what was left of the bowl, his whiskey-colored eyes taking in every piece, as though he knew exactly where each of the bits fit together.

"We can fix it," Beth said quickly. "I'll have Curry find some glue, and we can put it back together again."

"No." Ian kept hold of Beth's hands.

"But we can *try*."

Ian finally looked at her, his mesmerizing gaze meeting hers for a brief instant before it slid away again. "No, my Beth. It won't be the same."

Tears slid down Beth's cheeks, and she reached again for the pieces. She would gather them up, paste the thing back together, try to find its beauty again.

A bite of pain made her jump. Ian lifted her hand and kissed a spot of blood on her thumb.

"Stay here," he said quietly.

He flowed to his feet, leather boots creaking, and walked swiftly out of the room. Beth waited, more tears coming, and she put her thumb into her mouth to stop the bleeding.

She couldn't believe she'd done this, ruined the thing Ian had wanted so much, had worked so hard to find. He'd finally won his heart's desire, and Beth had broken it.

She had to fix it. She had to. If she couldn't repair the bowl, she'd have to find another one. The Russian gentleman might have a similar bowl, or know someone who had. She'd need help—and she knew just which Mackenzie she would recruit to help her. Hart could make the world turn upside down and shake out its pockets if he truly wanted to, and Beth would explain that he truly wanted to. This was for Ian.

Ian returned, carrying a broom and a dustpan. He put out his hand to stop Beth when she tried to climb to her feet, then Lord Ian Mackenzie, youngest brother of the Duke of Kilmorgan, swept up the tiny shards of porcelain and shoved them into the dustpan.

"What the devil?" Curry ran into the room, taking in Ian then Beth on the floor. "M'lady, what happened?"

He asked Beth, because Curry knew that if Ian didn't choose to answer, he wouldn't.

"I broke the bowl," Beth said, miserable.

Ian carried the broom and dustpan to Curry. "Throw the pieces away."

"Just like that?" Curry bleated. "*Throw the pieces away?*"

Ian gave him an impatient look, shoved the dustpan and broom into Curry's hands, and turned for the open door.

"Where are you going?" Beth called after him.

Ian glanced back at Beth but didn't meet her gaze. "Jamie and Belle will be awake from their naps in five minutes."

Because Ian knew his son's and daughter's routines by heart, and never let anyone vary them, he would be right.

Beth didn't relax. "Tell them I'll be up soon," she said.

Ian nodded once and walked away.

Beth got to her feet, picking a minute piece of porcelain out of her skirt.

Curry stared at her, round-eyed, still holding the dustpan. "What happened?"

"I don't know. It slipped out of my hands." Beth dropped the last piece into the dustpan, her breath hurting as she spoke. "Oh, Curry, I feel so very awful."

"No, m'lady, I mean, what did 'e *do*?"

"He . . . fetched a broom and swept up the pieces. But I could see he was upset."

"That's all?"

"I wouldn't say that was *all*. He had trouble looking at me, and I know I've hurt him. He wanted that bowl so much."

Curry turned away, laid the dustpan next to the opened box, and propped the broom against the table. "'E broke another bowl once," he said in a slow voice, "about a year before 'e first clapped eyes on you. It were 'orrible, m'lady. Screaming like . . . I've never 'eard a sound like that come out of a 'uman throat. Me and Lords Mac and Cameron had to sit on 'im to keep 'im from 'urting 'isself. 'Is Grace wasn't 'ere — off politicking at the time — but 'Is Grace had to come back from wherever 'e was to calm Lord Ian down. It were days to get 'im to quiet, and none of us slept a wink."

Beth listened, disquieted. She'd seen Ian in what he called his "muddles," when he lost control of his rage or performed an action over and over, desperately trying to make sense of whatever had happened to set him off. But he'd not done that in years, not since their marriage ceremony in their cozy house not far from here. Beth's domestic life so far had been nothing short of blissful.

Ian had broken Beth's heart the night she'd met him, when he'd explained that he had no ability to love, had no idea what love felt like.

He'd since proven he *did* know how to love — he proved it every day.

"Ian's become quite good at controlling his rages," Beth said, but the words didn't come out with the conviction she'd hoped they would.

"Aye, and we all breathe a sigh of relief, we do, knowing you're looking after 'im. But this were a Ming bowl. Maybe 'e's just 'olding it in."

"He'd never let himself go into one of his muddles in the nursery. He'd never do anything to hurt the babies." Her conviction was firmer now.

"If ye recall, 'e didn't actually say 'e were going to the nursery. 'E only said the kiddies were finishing their naps."

Beth and Curry shared a worried look, then both of them rushed to the door. At the last minute, Curry stepped back to let Beth exit first, then they hurried down the hall and up the long staircase to the huge nursery the cousins shared when the family gathered.

Nanny Westlock, who considered herself in charge of the rest of the nannies, looked up from her darning in surprise as Beth and Curry ran inside the sunny room.

Near one of the wide windows, Ian was just lifting Belle out of her cot. Two-and-a-half year-old Jamie had already headed for the large wooden rocking horse he'd received from Cameron for his second birthday.

Ian set Belle on the floor and held her little hands while she walked eagerly toward Beth. "Mama!" she said brightly. Ian slowed his giant steps for her, his boots alongside her chubby legs.

"Look at me, Mama!" Jamie yelled from the horse. "Like Uncle Cam."

"Excellent, Jamie," Beth said. "Uncle Cameron says you have a good horseman's seat." She lifted Belle as Belle dropped Ian's hands and raised her arms for her mother.

Ian put his hand on Belle's back, Ian always worried that the little girl would fall. Beth hugged her close, determined to prove she wouldn't drop *this* precious package at least.

Ian met Beth's gaze and gave her one of his rare, full smiles. No pain lingered in his eyes, only the warmth he showed when he was in the nursery. The bowl might never have been broken.

"Yes, Mr. Curry?" Nanny Westlock said as Curry lingered in the doorway. "May I be of assistance?"

"Just going, Miss Westlock. Ye run your kingdom to your 'eart's content."

Miss Westlock only gave him a look, but Curry grinned at Beth and shut the door behind him.

Ian moved to Jamie and started showing him how to hold the reins between his small fingers. Jamie was already tall for his age and robust. He'd be a towering Mackenzie before long.

Beth cuddled Belle in her arms and watched her husband become absorbed in his children. She hoped Curry would take the broken pieces downstairs, but she'd have to worry about the bowl and what to do about it later.

THE AT LEAST TWENTY PEOPLE IN THE SERVANTS' HALL listened in horror and then surprise as Curry related his tale. John Bellamy, his blunt fingers working a needle to repair the lining of one of Lord Mac's riding coats, listened while Curry spoke with his usual flair for dramatics. Curry finished by dumping the contents of the dustpan across the table, what was left of a very expensive Ming bowl.

"'Er ladyship wants it put together again," Curry finished. "So 'ow 'bout it?"

The servants around the table leaned forward, white caps and dark and light heads bent as hands reached for the pieces and started sorting.

Bellamy stayed out of it, his hands with their ill-healed broken fingers not good for lifting delicate things like shards of porcelain. A needle and thread was about as nimble as he could get. He usually asked a maid to help him with mending Lord Mac's clothes, but there was so much to do to ready the house for Christmas that he didn't feel it right to bother them.

As he watched the others start fitting pieces together and arguing about what went where, he again thought about his decision to retire. Lord Mac should have a younger man, one more like the suave Marcel who waited on the duke, instead of a broken-down former pugilist.

Lord Mac's lady wife was looking after him fine now. No more did Bellamy need to lift a limp and drunken Lord Mac, undress him like a child, and put him to bed.

Bellamy was nearing forty, and he'd been in one too many fights. He'd worked for a crooked fight manager who'd staged every one of Bellamy's matches, but that didn't mean the punches hadn't been real.

Time for him to move on. He'd run a pub, or he'd train young boxers and teach them how to avoid working for outright thieves.

Wouldn't be easy to tell Lord Mac, though. Lord Mac's feelings would be hurt, but Bellamy knew that his lordship didn't truly need him anymore.

Feeling slightly sad, Bellamy laid aside his mending and left the hall, seeking the back door. He heard the others' exclamations of surprise when Curry explained that Lord Ian *hadn't* had one of his fits when the bowl broke, but Bellamy was not amazed. Lord Ian had been a changed man since he'd married little Mrs. Ackerley.

There was another reason Bellamy wanted to go. He was lonely.

Outside, all was dark, and freezing. The sun had gone, night coming swiftly this far north. Bellamy's breath fogged out, and his feet crunched on the frozen ground. No snow at the moment, but it was coming.

He walked around the corner of the kitchen wing, out of the wind. He heard a gasp, saw another fog of breath, and stopped. At his feet crouched a bundle of clothes. Not rags—the person inside had piled on as many layers as possible against the cold.

A face inside a hood stared up at Bellamy, terror in her eyes flaring as she took in his height and breadth.

"Please," she said. "Don't make me move on yet. Just a while longer, out o' the wind."

Her accent wasn't broad, but it put her from right here in the Highlands. Bellamy had never seen her before.

"Who are you?"

Bellamy's voice came out harsh and scratched. His east London accent couldn't be reassuring either.

The woman flinched, but she held on to her courage. "I'm no one. But please, if you could spare a bit of bread before I go."

Bellamy reached for her. She cringed away, as though expecting a blow, but Bellamy held his hand to her, palm out. "Come with me."

The woman started to scramble to her feet. "No, I'll

move on. I know he's a duke and all. I never meant
no harm."

Bellamy seized her by the arm, clamping down when
she made to jerk away. "Don't be daft, woman. I meant
ye need to come inside and get warm."

She stared up at him in more fear, then resignation.
This poor lass probably hadn't had a word of kindness in
a long while, and when she had, she'd likely had to pay
for it.

Bellamy felt a bite of anger at whoever had made her
pay in the past. Well, she'd understand soon enough that
not all was darkness. He led her into the echoing hall
behind the kitchens and closed the door against the
night, all thoughts of retiring pushed aside for the
moment.

ELEANOR, THE DUCHESS OF KILMORGAN, LAY IN THE
warm bliss of her bed, while her husband placed another
slow kiss on her swollen abdomen.

This had been one of the difficult days, when she'd
only been able to rise to toddle to the necessary and back
again. And she had to use the necessary so often these
days. Her three sisters-in-law assured her this was
normal, but Eleanor worried. She was thirty and having
her first child. She knew there was danger, and Hart
did too.

The duke kissed her again, adding a brush of tongue.
He lifted his head, Hart's eyes deep golden in the
shadows.

"You are the most beautiful thing I've ever seen," he said in his low, rich voice.

Eight months of marriage hadn't dimmed Hart's passion. In fact, their marriage was awakening desires he'd kept long buried. Eleanor learned more about Hart every day she lived with him.

Eleanor smiled as she laid her hand on her belly, feeling a tiny movement within. "I am very rotund."

"Beautiful," Hart repeated firmly, a spark lighting his eyes. He liked to be commanding.

"Carrying your child," she said. "I'm very happy to."

Hart slid a little way up the bed and touched a kiss to her equally swollen breasts. They ached, but his kiss soothed.

Eleanor was naked, surrounded by blankets and pillows, and the fire in the white and gold stove was stoked full of coal. She must be the warmest person in the house.

Hart had returned from the funeral a little bit ago and come to her—cold, disgruntled, his face hard. He'd undressed near the stove, boots, coat, and cravat coming off impatiently, shirt following them to the floor. He'd stripped out of his underbreeches, leaving his kilt in place, then climbed up on the bed with her, laying Eleanor down and kissing her before he'd spoken a word.

Seeking comfort. Eleanor was happy to give it. Hart had suffered much loss in his life, had sacrificed so much, more than anyone but Eleanor understood.

Hart told her about the funeral while he lay against her, having skimmed off her nightrail. He touched her with

the possessiveness of a husband, the tenderness of a lover.
They'd talked, voices low, until his bleak look had gone.
Hart hadn't been great friends with Mrs. McCray or her
husband—far from it—but the funeral had stirred memories of his father and the rather horrible man he'd been.

"Not long now," Eleanor said, her chubby fingers
tracing the movement on her abdomen. "Thank heavens.
I look forward to walking about my own house again.
Without the waddling."

CHAPTER THREE

*L*augher tinged Hart's voice. "You don't waddle."

"Mac said I looked like a mother duck. And he is right, blast the man."

"I'll speak to Mac."

"Don't bother. I shook my finger at him. But the comparison was apt. I caught sight of myself in the mirror. Still, 'twill be a nice Hogmanay gift, do you not think? A little boy to dandle on your knee?"

"Or a girl."

"We've had this argument many a time. He will be a boy."

"Mackenzies do as they please. So do Ramsays." Hart ran his hand across her lower abdomen and around her navel.

"I know they do. Which is how I know he is a boy. Did you wager on a girl in Daniel's pool?"

Hart sent her a glance laced with heat. "Do you think I would wager on the outcome of my own child?"

"Danny's become quite the little bookmaker, has he not? I of course put down twenty pounds on boy."

"Only twenty? I thought you were so sure of the outcome."

"It's a frivolous wager, and one should not set a bad example. Besides, Daniel is drawing a large commission. I asked what he needed the money for, and he said he was building things. I shudder to imagine his flat in Edinburgh—loaded to the brim with mechanical parts and gears and oddities, I shouldn't wonder."

"I don't know. He lets no one in." Hart skimmed his hand down to her thigh, his fingers gentle but skilled. He moved to the foot of the bed and knelt there, kilt spreading over his large thighs. "Lie back. I'll rub your feet."

"Mmm." Eleanor wriggled her toes as Hart took her heel in his hand. "Every princess wants this in her Prince Charming. He rides up to the castle, kisses her awake, and rubs her aching feet."

Hart pressed soothing circles into the ball of Eleanor's foot, and she hummed in pleasure. Even more so when Hart leaned down and licked across her arch.

Hart had taught Eleanor pleasures she had never heard of, and she knew he'd only touched upon his vast knowledge. He feared to shock her or hurt her, but Eleanor was teaching him that she was made of stern stuff.

He'd continued to make love to Eleanor as she'd been increasing, up until the last month, when everything, including walking, had become painful. Even then, Hart had known how to make her feel good.

She'd learned this year about the erotic touch of silk

or feathers on skin, how a blindfold could heighten those feelings, how the whisper of Hart's breath in intimate places could render her body open and ready for him. He'd touched every inch of her with light strokes or with the weight and pressure of his hands, until she was coming apart in pleasure.

He hadn't done much with restraints once her body had begun thickening, but Hart had continued stirring her excitement by brushing her with the tethers of silk and leather. Eleanor shivered now, thinking on it.

"Lie still," Hart said in a low voice, but one that held steel. "Let me look after you."

Eleanor forced her body to relax. She really shouldn't —she had a million things to do to prepare the house for the holiday celebrations, and she couldn't expect Ainsley, Isabella, and Beth to do everything for her.

But Hart's touch, his voice, made her sink down among the pillows. He lifted away, and she heard a clink of glass on glass, smelled the warm perfume of oil. Hart ordered oils from Paris, and he'd made her choose her favorite scents from a very discreet shop when they'd traveled to France in the summer.

Mmm, vanilla and a touch of spice. Eleanor kept her eyes closed and inhaled as Hart smoothed his hand around her ankle. He slid his fingers up her calf and behind her knee, kneading a little, before he returned his attention to her right foot.

He pressed his thumbs into her arch and onto the ball of her foot, the oil and his touch easing tension. He gave pleasure to each of her toes, smoothing them, rubbing, pinching the slightest bit.

He pressed her heel against his bare chest and gently

rotated her foot, holding her toes while he eased her swollen ankle. Lowering her foot to the mattress, Hart held it lightly with one hand while he slid his other hand up her leg to her inner thigh.

His fingers lingered just below the join of her legs, his eyes warm as he watched her. He stroked his thumb over the inside of her thigh, not touching her more intimate places, but coming very close. The whisper of air he stirred, the stroke of his oiled fingers, made Eleanor let out a slow breath.

She started to move, lifting to his touch, but Hart pressed her firmly back to the mattress. "No, love. Stay still. I'll do everything."

Eleanor let herself sag again. Difficult when Hart's touch, light yet confident, sent ripples of hot pleasure through her body.

She'd learned not to fight him. To fight him brought out his wicked side—the feral smile, the look in his eyes that would frighten a lesser woman. Sometime, when she was feeling brave, Eleanor deliberately disobeyed him, to see what he'd do.

And the things he'd do . . . He'd become firm, no longer tender, tie her wrists with a cravat, or fasten her hands to the bed, or roll her over and chastise her backside. It would start as a game, and then Eleanor, who prided herself on her presence of mind, would become a begging pile of emotion. She'd dissolve into pure pleasure, crying his name, pleading for him, hearing his dark laughter, the bite of his teeth in her flesh, the sting of his hand.

He'd been kind to her, Hart said, during her pregnancy, but he promised he was storing up all sorts of things for later.

For now, his touch was light, warm, tracing pleasure onto her skin. He circled his thumbs over her inner thigh, just brushing the curls at the join of her legs. One finger flicked her opening, so sensitive now. She dragged in a breath, then another even more sharp as Hart leaned down and kissed where he'd touched.

His breath tickled her skin, hotter than his hands. The cool of the wedding ring on his left hand contrasted the heat, making her remember the intoxicating moment when she'd slid it onto his finger.

A knock at the door made Hart's body tighten, but he never roughened his touch on Eleanor.

"Your Grace," a faint voice came through the wood. "It is Wilfred."

Hart said nothing, but the soft light left his eyes, angry hardness filling them. No one, but no one, disturbed the duke when he was alone with his wife.

"Poor Wilfred," Eleanor said. "You'd better see what he wants. He would never dream of bothering you if the matter weren't terribly important."

Hart heaved a long sigh. He pressed a kiss to the inside of Eleanor's knee, got himself off the bed without jostling her, snatched up his shirt, and dragged it on as he went to the door in it and his kilt.

He jerked the door open only enough to slide out and close it again, never letting Wilfred catch a glimpse of Eleanor in the bed.

Eleanor rested her hand on her abdomen as she waited impatiently. Drat her uncooperative body. She was dying to know what Wilfred had to say, but she couldn't rise from the bed to find out.

A long time passed before Hart returned, keeping the door partway closed as he entered. He turned the key in the lock, then paused to skim off his shirt and unpin his kilt, letting the plaid fall to the floor.

Naked, gloriously so, Hart climbed back onto the bed, again not disturbing Eleanor, and snuggled down in the covers next to her.

"Well?" Eleanor asked when he remained silent. "Tell me at once, before I go mad."

Hart deliberately settled the covers around both of them, ending up resting his elbow on Eleanor's pillow, his hand on hers on her abdomen. He took another minute or so after that, simply looking at her, before he spoke.

"Beth broke the bowl."

"Oh, no." Eleanor sat up, or as upright as she could. Hart didn't have to explain which bowl. "What happened? Is Ian all right? Is Beth?"

"Apparently, Ian took it in stride. Beth is more upset, from Curry's reports."

"Well, she would be. How awful." Eleanor started to push back the sheets. "We must make sure she's all right."

Hart stilled her with a strong hand. "*You* must stay here and rest. Beth and Curry have things in hand, and Ian is with his children."

"And he's not . . ."

"He hasn't done anything at all, Wilfred said. Don't worry, love." Hart pressed a kiss to her lips, his body curving around hers protectively. "We'll watch him, and make sure all is well."

"We must find him a new bowl. One just like it."

"So Beth says." Hart softened enough to give Eleanor a smile. "She already told Wilfred I am to assist. I hear and obey."

"Because you're worried about Ian too."

"Yes." His smile vanished. "I am. The last time this happened it was a bloody disaster, and I was no help at all." He closed his eyes, shutting out remembered pain. "I hated that Ian wouldn't respond to me. I'm one of the most powerful men in Britain, I have foreign princes afraid to cross me, and I couldn't reach my own brother."

Eleanor stroked his hair, the warm silk of it soothing. She'd seen his frustration and hurt when he looked at Ian, great worry, and love.

"Ian's much better now. He has Beth."

"I know." Hart opened his eyes again, trying to hide his pain, but Eleanor always saw it.

"You'll find another bowl," Eleanor said with confidence. "You know so many people, and I'm certain they all owe you favors."

"They do. And I will."

"*After* you finish my foot rub."

Hart's smile returned, and with it, a glint of wickedness. "You're a demanding thing."

"Greedy." Eleanor ran her finger down his nose and tapped its tip. "Hungry for you. And sore."

Hart pressed a hot, open-mouthed kiss to her lips. "I'll give you your foot rub. But *my* way."

He ran his hand down to her thigh, fingers doing their dance on her sensitive skin. Eleanor leaned back on the pillows and gave herself over to the very talented ministrations of her husband.

ISABELLA MACKENZIE FINISHED WRITING YET ANOTHER letter the next evening, and stretched her aching fingers. The windows in her private sitting room were dark, and the air had turned frigid, though the coal stove kept her toasty warm.

Planning the large holiday festivities was a long and tedious process, but she, Ainsley, and Beth were determined to make Hart and Eleanor's first Christmas together memorable. The Scots, Isabella had learned from years of being married to one, didn't pay as much attention to Christmas Eve and Day as they did Hogmanay—New Year's. However, Hart had two English sisters-in-law and often had a houseful of English guests who expected Christmas crackers, plum pudding, and feasting on Christmas Day. Therefore, they had to plan two large celebrations, one at Christmas, one for Hogmanay, and yet another for Twelfth Night.

Isabella wanted this Christmas to be memorable for Eleanor in a good way. Some past Mackenzie Christmases had been out-and-out disasters, most of which had been caused by Mac's drunken debauches and his and Cameron's equally debauched friends. Half of these friends had ceased to be welcome at Kilmorgan—any Mackenzie household—after they'd decided it amusing one year to lock Ian into an attic room.

Isabella shuddered at the memory. Hart had been livid, and he and Cameron had had a punch-up, Hart blaming Mac for the friends' antics, Cameron defending Mac, who could barely stand up from a hangover. Only Isabella's persuasion had kept Hart from slinging his two brothers out into the snowy night.

This year, the house would be full of rejoicing. Babes filled the nursery, more family and friends would pour in on them soon, and the Mackenzie men were . . . well, not exactly *tamed*. But at peace with themselves, no longer fighting life.

Ian's broken bowl was on everyone's mind, however. He'd said not a word about it, appearing at breakfast with Beth as composed as ever. Beth's flushed face and little smile told Isabella how Beth might have been soothing him, but the brothers were still worried.

She felt Mac's presence behind her before two strong arms came around her, and Mac's lips brushed a warm kiss to the curve between her neck and shoulder. The scarf that he wore over his hair when he painted touched her cheek.

"What are you doing out of your studio?" Isabella asked. Mac had retreated there after breakfast and hadn't been seen since. He still wore his painting kilt and boots, though he'd donned a shirt. Most of the time when painting, he didn't bother with the shirt. "Has something happened?"

"Yes, Nanny Westlock. Time for the children's tea. I was taken to task for not returning them to the nursery, and I came to you for comfort."

"And as you can see, I'm swimming in plans for Hart's Christmas ball and New Year's celebration."

"Isn't that what Wilfred is for?"

Isabella reached for another sheet of paper, Mac's

arms still around her. "Wilfred is a man and what I have in mind needs a woman's touch. Eleanor is fragile, and I like doing this for her."

"I know you do, love. You have a generous heart."

He kissed her again, and Isabella closed her eyes, momentarily consigning plans for Christmas, Hogmanay, and the coming year to oblivion. She'd fought long and hard to reconcile with Mac. She wanted to savor every moment she had with him, to erase the years she'd had to do without him.

"Daniel telegraphed," Mac said. "Cam's out, so the majordomo handed the telegram to me. He'll be arriving tonight."

"Excellent." Isabella opened her eyes, smiling in true enjoyment. "I miss having him underfoot. He's all grown up now."

"He's quick-witted, resourceful, inventive, and as stubbornly obsessive as any of us. Very dangerous."

"And yet, he'll still be the little boy who mistook me for your fancy lady the day after we married. Poor thing. He wasn't to know you'd brought an innocent miss into your house."

Mac's arms tightened around her. "Love, you'll never know how hard I fell for you, my haughty debutant, when I saw you in the middle of that ballroom, all lace and fineness. You looked at me, the great Mac Mackenzie, and I knew I was lower than worms."

"I was an arrogant little thing, so certain I was the catch of the Season. You brought me down a peg or two. I needed it."

"I never meant to bring you as far down as I did."

Mac's voice went low, and Isabella remembered the pain and heartache of the first years of their hasty marriage.

"We were both young, impatient, and selfish," she said softly. "It was bound to go wrong."

"Whereas now we are old, wise, and staid?" He nibbled her neck. "I hope we have some wickedness still in us. How about I send Bellamy for some scones and tea?"

Isabella flushed bright red, remembering one afternoon in her London house, when she'd shared scones and clotted cream with Mac for the first time since their separation. Her behavior had been decidedly *un*-ladylike.

"Perhaps," she said, the word demure, her gaze cast down.

Mac growled. "My little Sassenach. Do ye know how much I love you?"

Small footsteps interrupted Isabella's intended answer. They turned to see Aimee, their adopted daughter, five going on six, watching them solemnly from the carpet.

Isabella rose, her love for Aimee flooding her. They'd rescued the poor girl from a madman, and she'd brought Isabella and Mac closer again.

Isabella went to Aimee and lifted her, reflecting sadly that she was getting too big for such things. She planted a kiss on Aimee's pink face. Mac joined them, his arms going around his wife and daughter.

"Why are you out of the nursery?" Isabella asked.

"Yes," Mac said. "You'll have Nanny Westlock hunting me, ready to put buckshot into my backside."

"Papa," Aimee said reproachfully. "Don't be so silly.

Nanny wants to find Gavina. I told her I'd ask her what you've done with her."

"Gavina?" Mac blinked. "She belongs to Cam. Why should I have done anything with her?"

"Because she likes to play in the studio with us, and Aunt Ainsley didn't return her to the nursery for tea. Nanny thinks you might have forgotten where you left her."

"I didn't leave her anywhere," Mac said. "If she's not with Ainsley, she must be with Cam somewhere."

"Uncle Cameron has gone to the pub. Would Uncle Cameron have taken her to the pub?"

"No . . ." Isabella began, then she stopped. With Cameron, anything was possible. She glanced out the dark window. "I'm sure she's only followed one of the dogs or fallen asleep." Isabella set Aimee on her feet and took her hand. Mac took Aimee's other hand, his wink at Isabella telling her they'd continue their discussion about scones later. "Come along, Aimee. Let's find her."

DANIEL MACKENZIE STEPPED OFF THE LAST TRAIN OF the night to Kilmorgan, settling his hat as the train puffed steam then chugged slowly up the track to its next destination.

"Master Daniel," the stationmaster said. "Welcome back. If you wait a few moments, my son will drive you up to Kilmorgan Castle."

"I'll walk," Daniel said. "I've been sittin' on trains since Edinburgh, and my legs, they need some stretching. Have the lad take my case, but I'll take a stroll through the village."

"Powerful cold night for a stroll, lad."

"Aye, but the warm pub is between here and there." Daniel grinned at the stationmaster, who'd been stationmaster for more than the entire eighteen years of Daniel's life.

The stationmaster chuckled, snatched up Daniel's one bag, said good night, and disappeared into the station. Daniel pulled his greatcoat closer and walked swiftly to the road that led to the village.

Coming home was always a mixed blessing. Christmases at Kilmorgan had become much better since Ian had married Beth, even better with Mac and Isabella now back to loving each other, and the best since his father had done the sensible thing and married Ainsley.

Now that Eleanor was Duchess of Kilmorgan, maybe Uncle Hart would stop behaving like a snarling bear. From what Cameron had said, since the marriage Hart had regained the more playful, lighthearted side of his youth—*God help us all,* Daniel's father had concluded.

This homecoming would be more interesting than others, that was certain.

On the other hand, Daniel was restless, tired of waiting for life to begin. He liked his studies at Edinburgh, but they didn't move quickly enough for him. He'd taken to slipping away to spend time with a middle-aged man who built crazy gadgets in his house, which had led to a few scrapes that Daniel hoped had not come to the attention of his father.

The one street through Kilmorgan was deserted, not surprisingly, because a cold wind cut through the huddle of houses and back out again. No snow yet lay on the ground, but it clung to the mountains and waited to pounce on the valleys.

With relief, Daniel opened the door of the pub and stepped into its welcoming warmth.

A large man holding a glass of ale in one hand and a lit cigar in the other lounged at a table between fireplace and door. He sat alone, though he'd cut off a conversation he'd been having with two men playing cards at a nearby table.

The man took several long drags of the cigar, blew out the smoke, and said, "Hello, son."

CHAPTER FOUR

*D*ad." Daniel lifted his hand to the regulars in the public house, men he'd known all his life.

Lord Cameron Mackenzie, next in line for the dukedom until Eleanor bore a son, sat comfortably in their midst. The locals had never minded Cameron or Mac coming in to drink, play cards or darts, and join in the conversation. They didn't mind Ian either, who'd drink and sit in silence the rare times he'd visited with his brothers, though Hart still made them a bit nervous.

An open box of cigars sat on Cameron's table, and from the acrid scents around him, many of the men here had dipped into it. Daniel's father was generous—these were expensive.

Daniel took one of the cigars, bit off the end, lit the cigar with a match from a box on the table, and sank down across from Cameron. He smiled over at the barmaid, who smiled back and started working the taps.

"Wasn't expecting you 'til next week," his father said in his rumbling baritone.

"Wasn't expecting to come so soon." Daniel blew out smoke. "But I thought it was time to leave Edinburgh."

Cameron's eyes glinted. "You owe someone money?"

"Naw, they owed it to me. And are being bad-tempered about it. But when I claim my clockwork numbers machine can add a string of figures faster than a human being, they need to believe me."

"Clockwork numbers machine, eh?" Cameron took a long draw on his cigar, following it with a swallow of bitter. "What professor is teaching you that?"

Daniel shrugged. "No professor. Something I'm looking into on me own."

Cameron emphasized his words with fingers holding his cigar. "You begged me to go to that university, Danny. You're taking the degree."

"Oh, I'll have it, don't you worry." Daniel smiled up at the barmaid as she set the ale in front of him. "How are you, Kirsten? No girls as fine as you in Edinburgh, that's the truth."

The barmaid Kirsten had very blond hair, large blue eyes, a ready smile, and a body that stopped a man in his tracks. She was a few years older than Daniel, but had been perfectly happy to teach him to kiss once upon a time. "Och, don't lie to me, lad," she said good-naturedly then moved back to the taps under the watchful eye of her father.

"Why aren't you at the house?" Daniel asked. "Billing and cooing with me sweet stepmama?"

"Ainsley, Beth, and Isabella are planning a grand Christmas and Hogmanay feasting. Including a ball or two, bonfires, banquets, and numerous other festivities. There are decorators, extra servants, supplies coming at all hours, the ladies making lists, running about, and chattering, always chattering."

Daniel took a sip of the ale. Not the best in the world, but it had a bite that told him he was home. "Ye fled for your sanity, did ye? Will stepmama be happy when she finds you gone?"

"She won't notice. Not for a while."

"What will you do to escape the madness tomorrow?"

"See to the horses. They don't need to become too soft."

Daniel smiled to himself. Cameron loved his race-horses and would use any excuse to head for the stables or paddocks.

But looking at him across the table, Daniel saw the change in his father. He still possessed his hard edge and a grating note to his voice, but a new light had softened his eyes.

Cameron Mackenzie had held himself away from the world for a long time. Oh, he caroused and wenched with the best of them, but no one got past his granite shell. Time was, Daniel's father wouldn't have cared what a woman was doing with her time when he wasn't with her—he'd go about his business and give no thought to her at all.

Now, though Cameron smoked and drank in this masculine haven, he was fully aware that he'd go home to Ainsley, that she'd give him her bright smile, and pull Cameron, a great bear of a man, down to kiss his cheek.

Good to see his father so happy.

Cameron sat in companionable silence, while Daniel

caught up on the local gossip. He let himself be enticed into a game of cards, winning hands and losing them. He was soundly beaten at darts, because he wasn't good at it, which he knew. He passed out the winnings with graciousness, and by that time, the publican was ready to close for the night.

Daniel walked side by side with his father, their breaths fogging out in the frosty night, the first flakes of snow falling when they reached the gates of Kilmorgan Castle. They said good night to the gatekeeper and his family and bent their heads to the wind for the last half mile to the house.

Kilmorgan was lit from top to bottom. Daniel and Cameron entered to find chandeliers blazing, the hall table filled with burning lamps instead of greenery, and the majordomo distributing the lamps to members of the household. All the servants were up, as were Daniel's uncles and aunts, including Eleanor, who clung to a newel post at the top of the stairs.

"What the devil?" Cameron shouted into the noise.

Hart turned to him, eyes blazing anger. "I was about to send someone to run for you."

Before Daniel could ask why, Ainsley cut through the crowd straight for Cameron, the myriad lights dancing on her fair hair. "Gavina is gone," she said, a frantic note in her voice. "We can't find her anywhere."

CAMERON'S WORLD STOPPED AND NARROWED TO HIS wife, her face smudged with dust, her gray eyes wide with fear, and her words: *We can't find her anywhere.*

Gavina, Cameron's pretty one-year-old daughter with hair of gold like her mother's—no, she couldn't be truly gone. Ever since she learned to walk, she'd been leading them a merry dance, often disappearing, but she'd always been easily found.

The knot in Cameron's stomach was nothing to the stark terror in Ainsley's eyes. Cameron ignored the throng around him and pulled Ainsley into his arms. The scent of roses touched him as he closed his arms around her shaking body.

"We'll find her, love." He kissed her hair. "She can't have gone far."

"But it's snowing. And so cold."

Cameron felt her panic. Ainsley had lost her first baby, the poor mite dying after only one day. That child had been called Gavina, and so Cam and Ainsley had named their first wee one in honor of her.

Gavina Mackenzie was robust and healthy, too robust sometimes. But Cameron understood Ainsley's fear and shared it.

"We've looked in all the likely places," Hart was saying. "Now we're combing the house top to bottom. Every nook and cranny—every single one, understand?" He pointed at groundskeepers. "You five and me, we'll cover the outbuildings. We all meet back here in an hour and report, sooner if she's found, of course."

The servants and household dispersed. Mac, still in his painting kilt with the red scarf over his hair, took Isabella's hand and led her up and up the stairs to the very top of the house.

Ainsley slid out of Cameron's arms, tears on her face.

"Go with Hart," she said, touching Cam's chest. "Find her. Please."

"I will, love." Cameron held Ainsley until the very last minute, then she rushed away after Isabella and Mac.

Daniel grabbed a lantern. "We'll find her. Don't you worry. Her legs are short. Difficult for her to walk a long way."

"Short but very, very fast." Cameron had seen Gavina totter down a hall with the speed of one of his thoroughbred colts, gone in the blink of an eye. Ainsley blamed herself, Cameron saw that.

And where was I? Cameron thought grimly. In the bloody pub. Like the old days. Not looking after my girl, just as I didn't look after my boy.

His boy now stood beside him, Cameron's same height if not his breadth, none the worse for Cameron's fatherly neglect. Daniel had gone missing regularly, Cameron remembered, at first wanting his father to come find him, and later wanting his father *not* to find him.

Daniel had been a lonely, neglected boy. No one could say that Gavina was neglected in any way — Cameron had been making sure of that. She'd wandered off, he told himself. She'd gone exploring and gotten lost.

In the dark, in the cold, with the snow coming down . . .

Cameron walked faster and faster, the other men with lanterns falling behind him. Only Daniel kept up.

"They say they already looked in the stables," Daniel said. "Where else does she like to go?"

"Everywhere," Cameron said darkly. "She likes the

gardens. Ainsley's not fool enough to let her go out there at night."

"I'm thinking stepmama did not exactly *let* her go anywhere."

Cameron growled to himself and kept walking. Gavina wasn't used to Kilmorgan—she'd been here only a couple of times since her birth, and last year at this time she'd been a tiny thing in a cradle.

This year, she'd been fascinated by Hart's big house, by the nursery she shared with her cousins, by the decorations her mother and aunts were strewing about the house, by the back halls and stairs that the servants traversed. She also liked the big, formal gardens with their maze-like paths and gigantic fountains. The fountains weren't playing now, but she'd liked the one of Apollo's chariot and horses. Gavina liked anything to do with horses and wasn't afraid of the beasts at all.

Damn it. If she'd decided to climb up on the horses at the fountain . . .

Cameron broke into a run, Daniel behind him. They reached the Apollo fountain in the middle of the garden within a minute, Cameron's heart hammering.

All was quiet. Cameron and Daniel flashed their lanterns, light gleaming on the icy marble of the horses, on the empty water spigots that spouted from beneath the chariot. Apollo the sun god stood upright, never minding the snow dusting his head and shoulders.

"She's not here," Cameron said with some relief. No little body lying on the ground after she'd toppled from the slippery horses or the chariot. "Why the devil doesn't Hart destroy this monstrosity of a fountain anyway?"

"Because it's by Bernini, brought over from Rome, and a masterwork of seventeenth-century engineering?"

"Shut it, boy. Where else?"

"Rest of the gardens? Stables?"

"Stables," Cameron said. "We'll check them again."

"She's a Mackenzie all right." Daniel said it lightly, but Cameron heard the worry in his tone.

They made their way back to the other men. The dogs had come to help too, except Ben, who'd walked slowly to the bottom of the terrace and sat down. He was old, and didn't like the cold.

The other dogs swarmed, tails moving, excited at the hunt. If any of them could be relied upon to track Gavina, Cameron would turn them loose. But the dogs were family pets because they weren't good at what they'd been bred for—retrieving birds or hunting, or even ratting in the case of Fergus. Hart refused to destroy an animal simply because it wasn't useful, so they became companions to the family.

Cameron strode for the stables, a vast line of buildings that housed Hart's horses and Cam's special racers, the tack rooms, the carriage houses, and the grooms' quarters. Searching every corner of the place would be as difficult as tackling the house.

Cameron, though, went through them, every stall, the grooms helping with the search. The little girl wasn't in the haylofts, or hidden in one of the carriages, or behind saddle trees in a tack room.

Cameron strode back into the yard, sucking cold air into his lungs. He could barely find breath, and it was so cold. Gavina couldn't have been wrapped up warmly; she might freeze to death before they found her.

God, no. Please. No.

What had he said only yesterday morning, walking home from the bleak churchyard? *Too many bloody funerals in this family already.*

Cameron had stood at a graveside on another cold winter day to bury his first wife after she'd taken her own life. He'd watched his mother go, his father, Hart's wife and little boy.

Not Gavina. Not her. If she died, it would break Ainsley. Ainsley would dissolve into grief, and Cameron wouldn't be able to help her.

Damn it, I can't lose them.

He found himself bent double, hands on knees, his lungs not working. A warm hand gripped his shoulder.

"Dad. Ye all right?"

Daniel. Daniel was his constant, the one person who'd made Cameron's life bearable all these years. Air poured back into him, and Cameron slowly stood up. Daniel's eyes, as golden as Cameron's, held fear.

"I'm all right, son. Just scared out of my mind."

"We'll find her. We will."

Cameron shook his head. "It's too bloody cold. There won't be time. She's so tiny."

The world was spinning around, but Daniel was there, his hand on Cameron's shoulder. Cameron would have to go into the house and tell Ainsley, have to watch the light go out of her eyes.

He couldn't do it. "We have to find her."

"Aye." Daniel's grip tightened. "We will."

Ruby, the hound who'd taken up residence with Ian and Beth, galloped by, followed by Ian himself, holding a lantern high.

"Where is Achilles?" Ian called to them.

Achilles was a setter, or at least, a partial one. He had jet black fur except for one white hind foot, which gave him his name. Cameron realized that he'd seen only four of the five dogs—Ruby, Fergus, and McNab running about, Ben waiting near the terrace—but he hadn't paid much attention.

"I don't know," Cameron snapped. "I'm more interested in finding my daughter."

Ian came to a halt and looked straight at Cameron— he'd become better at meeting his brothers' eyes in the last few years, even though he sometimes still found it difficult. At the moment, his gaze held Cameron's.

"We need to look for Achilles."

"Damn it, Ian . . ."

"No, wait," Daniel said. "I think Uncle Ian's got it. I haven't seen Achilles since we arrived home, and Gavina likes him. What's more, he likes her." Daniel's eyes sparkled with excitement, the lantern making his face sharp.

Cameron's breath came faster as he raised his lantern and flashed it around the stable yard. Achilles did follow Gavina with devotion, and the little girl might have felt safe going outside with him. Gavina might not be able to answer their calls, but Achilles would.

"Sorry, Ian," Cameron said. He found himself saying that to Ian quite a bit. "I didn't understand."

Ian gave him a faint nod but didn't answer. His look told Cameron that he knew his older brother was an idiot, but he'd learned to put up with it.

"Hart!" Cameron moved to catch up with the bulk of the duke and explain.

Soon men were bellowing into the night, *Achilles! Where are you, lad?* The other dogs, recognizing the name, started barking in earnest.

The trouble was, they now were making so damn much noise that Cameron couldn't hear a blasted thing. He broke away from the main group, Daniel close behind him.

Cameron went out into the dark, away from the teeming stable yard. The musty scent of horses came to him on the wind, the cold of the night stealing his breath.

The wind cut out on the leeward side of the stables, the relative warmth a waft of relief. Faint and faraway, Cameron heard the loud *arf arf* of the one dog that wasn't there.

He stopped, and Daniel almost ran into him, lantern swinging. They both froze, listening.

It came again, the frantic barking of a dog trying with all its might to get their attention.

Cameron walked swiftly toward the sound, down the length of the back of the stables, its long stone wall rising high beside him.

"There!" Daniel said, pointing.

At the end of the wall, boards had been nailed over a hole to protect the crumbling foundation. From behind it was the unmistakable barking of Achilles—starting low and ending high, in almost a squeak. The more excited Achilles became, the squeakier he sounded.

The high-pitched barking escalated, accompanied by the noise of paws scrabbling on wood. Cameron and Daniel dropped to their knees, lanterns clanking on the ground, both men reaching at the same time for the gray pieces of board. Two pairs of gloved hands, one huge, the other thinner and more wiry, yanked wood away from the hole.

Achilles' snuffling nose came into view, his body squirming as his tail wagged deep inside the hole. Daniel got his hands around the dog and started pulling him out. Cameron didn't let himself think about the fact that Achilles might have become stuck down here by himself, nothing to do with Gavina.

Daniel fell back, his arms full of the dark-furred Achilles. Achilles, panting in happiness, licked Daniel's face, then went right back into the hole.

CHAPTER FIVE

amn you, dog!" Daniel shouted and grabbed for him again.

Achilles filled the hole for a brief instant, then he squeezed on inside, his hindquarters writhing with his wagging tail.

Cameron's lantern fell on a confusion of objects behind the dog, some small and squirming, little peeping noises issuing from the dark. Cameron saw the wide reflective eyes of a cat, and beyond that, a flash of pink.

Somewhere in the back of his whirling thoughts, Cameron remembered Angelo, his groom, friend, and valet, telling him that cats always instinctively sought the warmest places to sleep. *If you seek warmth, find a cat.*

Cameron yanked loose another board and started to put his head inside the hole. Daniel seized him by the shoulder.

"Let me, Dad. You'll get stuck."

Cameron, the largest Mackenzie, had to concede. He moved out of the way but stayed on his hands and knees while Daniel got himself on his stomach and slithered inside.

Cam heard a low *miaow* then Daniel's voice as he spoke to dog and cat. Daniel inched his way back, his kilt catching on the icy stones and exposing his thighs, but he didn't release the bundle he carried with him.

In a new pink dress her Aunt Eleanor had given her, topped with the tiniest rabbit fur coat Cameron had ever seen, Gavina was just opening her gray eyes, her face flushed with sleep. Achilles scrambled out behind her and ran to greet the other dogs coming up with the rest of the men, led by Ian and Hart.

Daniel sat back, lifted Gavina to his lap, and blew out his breath. "She's lovely warm. Probably stayed warmer than any of us tonight."

Gavina blinked sleepy eyes at her stepbrother and father, then lifted her arms. "Dabby," she said.

"I'm here, sweetie." Cameron scooped up Gavina with his giant hands and cradled her against his chest, brushing the top of her head with his shaking lips. Her body was indeed warm, her breath milk sweet as she turned her face up to kiss his cheek.

"She was talking to me," Daniel said beside him. "She said *Danny*."

Cameron shook his head. "No, she said *Daddy*."

Father and son shared a stubborn look. Gavina pulled away from Cameron and reached for Daniel, her little hands opening and closing. Cameron relinquished her, and Daniel swung her up over his head, making her laugh.

"Who's the sweetest little sister a lad ever had, eh?"

Daniel said. "What were you doing out here, worrying us all to death?"

"Kitties." Gavina pointed back under the stables. The mother cat and kittens, perfectly happy where they were, looked out at the sudden influx of Scottish men and dogs with mild curiosity.

Cameron heaved himself to his feet, taking Gavina from Daniel and holding her close. His heart wouldn't stop hammering.

Daniel leaned the boards back over the hole, and Achilles danced in tight circles around first Cameron then Daniel. He ran to the other dogs, paused to touch noses with Ruby, and leapt back to Cameron again.

Hart lifted his lantern, the relief on his face undisguised. "You've got her, then."

"She's all right," Cameron said, barely able to form the words. "She's all right."

Ian was next to Hart, looking over Cameron, Gavina, Daniel, and the now-covered hole. Achilles ran to Ian, circling his legs.

Ian bent down and stroked the black fur. "Good dog," he said.

"You've found her?" Isabella leaned over the stair railings, Beth beside her, as the men and dogs swarmed back into the front hall.

Cameron held up a bundle of pink and fur, and Gavina squealed with laughter. Isabella clutched the railing, relief making her knees weak. Beth let out a shaky breath. "Thank God," she whispered.

Ainsley came out of the opposite wing, lifting her skirts as she flew down the stairs toward her husband and child. She was weeping as Cameron caught her up, crushing Gavina and Ainsley into a hug. Daniel put his arm around his father, leaning his forehead on Cameron's shoulder. Isabella's eyes stung as she watched the family pull into itself, the four of them comforting and rejoicing together.

Mac came down the stairs, two at a time, reaching Beth and Isabella. He hadn't taken the time to change out of his painting things, which was fine with Isabella. He looped one arm around Beth and the other around Isabella, kissing his wife's cheek.

"All is well, then," he said.

"Yes, thank heavens." Isabella leaned into Mac's embrace, loving that she could now be with him in relief. "Poor Ainsley. We should give her some tea, perhaps with whiskey."

"Splendid idea," Beth said, though her gaze was all for Ian, coming in with the rest of the dogs behind Hart.

"No, ye ladies can leave her alone to Cam and her babe," Mac said. "Danny will take care of them."

Hart, below, directed the housekeeper, Mrs. Desmond, to take everyone who'd searched to the dining room where they could enjoy whiskey and a light repast. Ever the generous host, Hart ushered them down the corridor himself. He looked impatient, though, wanting to return to Eleanor.

Ian didn't follow the others, but came straight upstairs to Beth. Not looking at Mac, Ian brushed his brother out of the way and caught Beth in an embrace.

"What happened?" Isabella asked him. "Where did you find her?"

Ian directed his answer to Beth. "Under the stables. With a cat. Achilles kept her safe."

"Thank God for our misbehaving and useless dogs," Mac said. "How on earth did she get under the stables?"

"That, I'm sure will be the question," Isabella said.

Below them, Cameron and Ainsley held each other, Gavina between them. Daniel rested his hands on their shoulders, speaking in a low voice.

"We should leave them to it," Beth said. "I for one, have the greatest desire to check again on my children."

"Indeed," Isabella said.

The two men didn't argue. The four mounted the stairs to the nursery, to find Nanny Westlock, already informed of Gavina's return, making sure the girl's bed was ready. Miss Westlock pressed a firm finger to her lips when the two couples came inside, indicating the sleeping children.

Isabella pulled a blanket a little straighter over Aimee, then smiled down at the dark red heads of Eileen and Robert, snug in their cots. Mac leaned down and pressed a kiss to all three children in turn, then led Isabella out.

Ian wouldn't leave, to Nanny Westlock's distress, and Mac laughed softly as he and Isabella went back to their wing of the house.

"Trust Ian to stand guard." Mac stopped on a shadowy landing and closed a comforting arm around Isabella. He smelled of paint and turpentine, and the heady scent of himself. Isabella sank into his warmth, her body shuddering in reaction. She'd shared Ainsley's fear, knowing what she'd feel if one of her own babies went missing.

Mac ran his finger under her chin, leaning down to kiss her. He tasted of spice and oolong tea, sweat and worry. But his stillness calmed her, as only Mac could.

Their lips met, and met again. Far away, the sounds of the household had turned joyous, laughter and raucous voices replacing the bowstring tension.

Mac's warmth flowed through his kiss, down through Isabella's body, loosening every limb. Isabella needed him, the reassurance that he was here and solid, protecting her and her children from harm.

Mac skimmed his fingertips over her cheek. "Let's seek someplace a bit more comfortable, eh, lass?"

Isabella smiled, loving his low voice and the promise in it. He put his arm around her waist, hand cupping, and led her on to their wing of the house.

Relief made Isabella giddy, wild need for Mac warming her blood. Instead of turning in at their bedchamber, as a decorous married woman ought, Isabella broke loose from Mac's hold and ran on up another flight of stairs to his studio.

In the early days of their marriage—and again when they'd first been reunited—they'd made love in Mac's studio, shamelessly naked on the couch, or on drop cloths on the floor. Young, innocent Isabella had learned to be wicked and wanton with the decadent Mac Mackenzie, and she wanted that wickedness tonight.

Mac vaulted past her, boots thumping, and put himself between Isabella and the studio door. "Where are you going?"

Isabella touched a paint splotch on his cheek. "I thought we could reminisce. You know, about old times."

Mac started to smile. He loved reliving their first days together, when he'd stolen her from her debut ball at her father's house, eloped with her that very night, and had her in his bed before dawn.

He deliberately erased the grin and pressed his back to the studio door. "Our bedchamber's warmer, my love."

"Your studio will be plenty warm, if Bellamy has had his way." Mac used to grow too absorbed in painting to feed the fire, but Isabella had put in place instructions for Bellamy to check it and stoke it if necessary.

"Bellamy will have gone to bed by now," Mac said. "Or joined in the repast. I imagine he's exhausted."

Isabella's eyes narrowed. He was speaking a bit too glibly. "Mac, why don't you want me to go inside?"

"Because I think the bedroom will be more comfortable, love, that's all. We'll want to sleep after, cuddle under warm blankets. Not be stiff and cold in the studio." He leaned his arm on the doorframe, blocking it.

"You are a bad liar, Mac Mackenzie."

Isabella darted under his arm, going for the doorknob and the key in the doorplate. Mac had his hands on her arms, whirling her around and pinning her to the wall next to the door before she saw him start to move.

He leaned to her, copper-colored eyes dark in the shadows. "A liar, am I? Thought I was a rogue."

He pressed Isabella against the wall, her bustle squashing against the molded trim of the wainscoting. Mac brushed her hair from her face with his thumb, then he drew back and gave her a slow smile, his eyes half closing.

"I've smudged paint on you." He brushed a kiss to her cheek, warming with his breath. "Remember, when you first came to my studio? We had paint up and down your arms, and found some on a very interesting place on my backside."

"At our house at Mount Street," Isabella said. Mac's studio had been at the very top of the house, their aerie away from the world. "I loved that room."

"As did I, lass." Mac touched another kiss below the paint smear then to her lips.

The kiss turned long, dark, passionate. Tongues flickered, lips met. Mac slid his hand up her waist to rest over her corseted breast.

Isabella wrapped one arm around her husband, palm going to his kilt-covered backside. He had such beauty, firm male flesh over a body of honed muscle. She loved to watch him paint, when he'd bare himself in all but his kilt and paint-speckled boots. His athletic body would move as he worked, sunlight kissing his skin and the faded plaid of his kilt. He'd pause, arm wiping sweat from his forehead, smears of paint decorating his face.

As she kissed him, Isabella let her other hand travel along the cool wall, walking with her fingers until she found the key in the door's lock.

CHAPTER SIX

A strong grip seized her and yanked the key out of her grasp. Mac took a step back, holding up the key, his smile triumphant.

"No, ye don't, Sassenach."

Isabella put her hands on her hips and let out an exasperated breath. "I went inside yesterday."

"I was ready for ye then." Mac backed away, holding the key out of her reach. "I'll let you in again when I'm done."

Her curiosity grew. "What is it, Mac? What are you hiding?"

"It's a surprise."

"You know I love surprises. Tell me now."

Mac laughed, the velvety sound she'd fallen in love with. "If I tell ye, it won't be a surprise, will it? You'll find out. Come Christmas."

"A Christmas present, is it?"

She walked toward him, hands behind her back, swaying a little. Mac studied her as she came, gaze raking from her pushed-forward breasts to her moving hips.

"Aye. The perfect gift, I'm thinking."

"What is it?"

"Can't tell you."

Isabella lunged for him. Mac whirled away, still clutching the key. He ran down the stairs, Isabella after him, then he made for a tall window on the landing and tucked the key on top of the cloth-covered cornice, well out of Isabella's reach.

She halted, her breath coming fast. "You know I can always ask Mrs. Desmond for the key."

"But you won't." Mac stepped to her again, slipping one hand around her waist and pulling her against him. "You'll save it for Christmas."

"I'll consider it."

"You will." Mac's face was an inch from hers, soft in the shadows. He gave her a slow kiss, full of desire.

"You're highhanded."

"I am, wife."

His mouth came to hers again, brushing fire. Isabella opened her lips for his, seeking him, wanting him. Mac had been able to make her crazed with need since the night she'd met him, when he'd strode so casually through the crowd at the ball in her honor, where he'd not been invited. Wild, daring Mac had turned her world upside down from that night to this.

He slid his hand to the nape of her neck, holding her, while he thoroughly kissed her mouth. He stepped into her, boot nudging between her high-heeled lace-up shoes.

Isabella hung on to him, her body pliant, knowing

he'd never let her fall. Never. Even when they'd been apart, those horrible years when they didn't speak to each other, Mac had been there, from afar, making sure she was all right.

He broke the kiss, his breath heating her skin. Isabella laced her fingers through his and tugged him along the hall to their bedchamber. She kissed him again as they nearly fell inside the door to the warm and welcoming room and its wide, embracing bed.

AINSLEY RESTED HER HAND ON GAVINA'S BACK, THE bassinet on its stand pulled near the big bed. She leaned her hip against the bed's mattress, unable to move from her daughter to get into the bed as Cameron had ordered her to.

Her daughter, her beautiful daughter, had nearly been lost. Gavina lay on her tummy in the bassinet, her head turned toward her mother, eyes closed in exhausted sleep. Ainsley reached out and smoothed one of the golden curls that tumbled over Gavina's cheek.

Cameron strode into the bedchamber with his usual energy, but he closed the door softly, not waking Gavina. Cameron's hair was damp, and he smelled of soap and also warmth under the dressing gown that covered him from neck to slippers.

"Ainsley." The mattress sagged as Cameron leaned on it next to her, his arm stealing around her, smoothing her nightgown. "Let Nanny Westlock take her. You need your sleep, little mouse."

"I should have been watching her," Ainsley said, the

pain of that welling like a fresh cut. "I shouldn't have taken my eyes off her for one moment."

Cameron was silent. His large body gave her comfort even through her sickening fear. He was the man who'd gone into the night and brought Gavina home.

"I had my hands full with this stupid Christmas celebration," Ainsley said. "Not noticing that my own daughter had gone missing, until it was too late."

"I was the one at the pub," Cameron said, his words heavy. "Throwing back a pint at the local was more important than looking after my family."

Ainsley gave him a surprised look. "This wasn't your fault."

"Why? Because fathers are supposed to be downing ale while the womenfolk carry on at home? Balls to that. I raised Danny on my own—I should know better than anyone that babies need your eyes on them all the time."

Ainsley heard the pain in his voice, the self-reproach. "I was arguing with Mrs. Desmond about the color of the tablecloths, when Nanny Westlock sent down word she didn't have Gavina. *The color of the tablecloths.* When my daughter . . ." Ainsley broke off, pressing a trembling hand to her mouth.

"Come here." Cameron pulled her against him, letting her head rest on his shoulder. His great strength came to her through his touch, and the heat beneath the dressing gown told her he was bare inside it. "Ye can't castigate yourself, love. Hart has an entire household of servants and nannies who were supposed to be looking after the children, not to mention my three brothers, their wives, and *their* servants. Someone should have seen her go, but none did. Danny's the only one guiltless in this—he was on the train."

"But I'm her *mother*," Ainsley said. "A bad mother."

"Stop." Cameron rumpled her hair. "You're hurting, love, I know, and not only about this."

Cameron knew her so well. He always had, even when he'd played the rakehell trying lure her—one woman out of many—into his bed. Cameron had understood when she'd told him about losing her first daughter. He'd been the only person in the world with whom Ainsley had been able to talk about that Gavina, the only one who'd held her until the pain lessened enough for her to bear.

Her terrible dread tonight was that any child given to her would come to harm, that God's plan for Ainsley didn't include her being a mother. Ainsley wasn't a stoic enough Scots to accept such a thing. She burned with fear, knowing that losing this Gavina would open a wound from which she might never recover.

"I can't stop thinking about her . . . out there alone . . . cold." Tears wet the soft velvet of Cameron's dressing gown.

"She wasn't cold, and she wasn't alone. She hadn't wandered aimlessly, she'd fixed on a purpose, a stubborn purpose, like the Mackenzie she is. Achilles went with her and protected her. He's going to be spoiled rotten after this . . ."

Ainsley had to smile as she looked across the carpet to the dog curled up by the fire. Everyone had certainly made a big fuss of Achilles when Daniel explained to all what had happened. Achilles was the hero of the hour, and Daniel suggested they fashion some kind of medal for him. The dog had been given a royal feast in the kitchen, but he'd followed Ainsley and Gavina back to Cameron's bedchamber, still guarding Gavina.

Cameron's arms came around Ainsley again, holding her close. "Hush now," he said, his voice gentle. "Hush, little mouse."

He'd called her that since the night he'd found her hiding in his bedchamber—this very one. Ainsley had been there for a perfectly good reason, in her opinion, nothing to do with Cameron. Cameron had caught her, growled at her, teased her, confused her, seduced her, then protected her and made her fall wildly in love with him.

Gavina was their love too, the little girl sweet and whole.

"As much as you're trying to make me feel better," Ainsley said. "I won't cease to blame myself."

"We're both to blame." Cameron's chest rumbled with his words. "The poor lass is cursed with us as parents. But it turned out all right, and we'll all three go on. She's taught us how diligent we need to be."

Ainsley raised her head. "Meaning she'll try it again. And again."

"Of course she will. She belongs to *this* family." Cameron tugged a lock of hair at his forehead. "Ye see these gray strands? That's all Daniel, that is. Had them before I was twenty-five."

Ainsley had to smile. "I imagine he was a handful."

"A handful, a fistful, an armful, an earful. Thank God I had brothers to help me and that they started getting married. I've been a rotten father, but Danny's muddled through."

"You're not a rotten father." Ainsley slid her hands to his shoulders. "Daniel has become a remarkable young man."

"Good God, don't tell *him* that."

"Don't tell me what?" Daniel swung the door open and walked inside, his wide smile broadcasting that he'd heard the last. "Are you crying, dearest stepmama? No need. We're all here, and safe."

"You walk into a bedchamber without knocking, Daniel Mackenzie?" Ainsley said, pretending indignation. "One with your *father* in it?"

"I knew there was no danger of embarrassing you as long as Gavina was here, not to mention the snoring dog. I came to fetch my baby sister, by the way. Nanny Westlock is demanding her return to the nursery, where she belongs. Her words, not mine. I offered to come down for her, so you wouldn't have to face the wrath of a nanny whose schedule has been disregarded. You may thank me with an extra helping of pud at Christmas dinner."

Daniel reached for the bassinet, which lifted from its stand by wicker handles.

"Perhaps she should stay here for the night," Ainsley said.

Daniel raised his brows. "Oh, so ye want to break *that* news to Miss Westlock, do you? She's in a rare temper as it is, blaming herself for losing track of Gavina. Every one of the maids and all the footmen are beating themselves blue for it too. The majordomo and Mrs. Desmond are each trying to outdo each other in self-blame, because they're responsible for all the rest of the servants. The only one sleeping well tonight is Gavina.

And Achilles. And maybe Eleanor. She almost dropped in her tracks from exhaustion, and Hart carried her up to bed. Hart's very angry, you can be sure. Oh, he blames himself too."

Cameron leaned to the bassinet to kiss his daughter's cheek. "Ye've managed to have the house in uproar, haven't you, love?" he asked her softly. "Just like your brother used to." He tickled Gavina's cheek, and Gavina stirred but didn't wake.

Ainsley drew a breath. "You're right, Daniel. Take her up to bed. I suppose she'll be safe enough in her cot. She won't get out of that."

"Actually, I used to . . ." Daniel broke off. "Ah. Never mind. Off to bed you go, my sweet little sister. Good night, stepmama." He leaned around Cameron and gave Ainsley a noisy kiss on her cheek.

"Do stop calling me that, Danny."

"Right you are. Good night, Father."

He went out with his usual energy. Achilles, awakened, trotted after them, tail moving. Daniel closed the door behind them, and quiet fell.

Cameron gathered Ainsley into his arms again. His heat came to her, and she heard the firm beating of his heart.

An ordinary man might say, *Come to bed, love. Everything will be fine in the morning.* But Cameron wasn't ordinary. She knew she wouldn't love him so much if he were.

Ainsley raised her head and kissed him.

His lips firmed against hers, the worry and fear in him changing to desperation. Ainsley tasted his hunger, the terror he'd shared with her.

Their child was safe, unharmed. This was a time to celebrate, not weep.

Ainsley wrapped her fingers around the lapels of his soft dressing gown and pulled it open. She found him bare inside, as she'd suspected, warm and still damp from his bath.

She skimmed her hands down his torso, his heartbeat quickening. His tight abdomen met her touch, his waist narrowing to his hips and the thickness of his cock.

"Don't." Cameron raised his head, gold gleaming from between half-closed eyelids. He seized her wrist, fingers shaking as he kept himself from gripping too hard. "Don't, unless you want me to . . ."

"She's safe," Ainsley whispered. "I want to rejoice."

Cameron smoothed her hair, his touch strengthening as he cradled her head in his hand. "Then we will," he said, voice rasping.

He dragged her to him, his next kiss anything but tender. Cameron opened her mouth, pressing her back. Ainsley tasted the need in him, the desire to hold on.

Her husband lifted her into his arms and laid her across the bed, coming down on top of her. A mad light gleamed in his eyes.

"Too confounded many buttons," he growled before he ripped her nightgown open from neck to waist.

Ainsley delved inside his dressing gown, wanting his skin touching hers. She loved the weight of his body on hers, comforting, protecting. Never hurting her. Cameron never would.

Cameron shed his dressing gown in impatient jerks and furrowed her hair with his hand. Pulling her head back, he kissed her—hard—and at the same time entered her.

His hands on her body were strong, kisses on her lips, her flesh, as strong. He loved her with firm, sure strokes, Ainsley opening to him, body rising to his.

Cameron loved her in silence tonight, speaking only with his body, his kisses, nips, touches. He stirred fire deep inside her to wash out the pain, the fear, the worry of everything to come.

He loved her until they were both crying out, peaking together, then falling again to the valley of peace, warmth, quietude. Cameron kissed her with the slow kisses of afterglow, their bodies sweating in the warm room.

"I love you, little mouse," Cameron said softly.

Then he gave her the sweetest gift he had to give—he curled up around her, pulled the covers over them, and went easily to sleep with her.

IAN ENTERED THE SITTING ROOM OF THE SUITE HE shared with Beth, looking forward to his warm bed and his wife in his arms. This last week with its chaos of preparations, the house swarming, and more and more people arriving had kept him unnerved. Ian had gown better at dealing with people around him, but that didn't mean he *liked* it.

Poor Gavina going missing tonight had given him something practical to do, a problem to solve. Ian was much better at that. Finding Achilles, her favorite dog, had seemed the obvious thing to do.

Cameron had looked intensely relieved when she was found, and in this instance, Ian found empathy. If one of *his* children had disappeared, Ian would have been frantic. Any thought of harm to Jamie or Belle made him physically ill. Ian had spent the last hour up in the nursery, watching his little boy and girl, until Nanny Westlock and Daniel, carrying in Gavina, had chased him out.

No matter. Ian would see the babies tomorrow. If the weather was fine, he'd take them out riding. Jamie was already a good rider, and Belle was learning quickly.

His thoughts dissolved when he beheld Beth sitting on the carved old-fashioned sofa, a book in her lap. The blue satin gown she'd worn for dinner was now rumpled and dust-stained, but it hugged her waist and bared an enticing glimpse of bosom. The bustle made her sit on the edge of the sofa, her satin skirts nearly hidden by the large book.

Ian recognized one of his texts on Ming bowls. He remembered the broken bowl and felt a pang of loss. It had been beautiful, and he'd only been able to hold it a few short moments.

But the bowl was nowhere near as beautiful as his wife, who looked up at him with sensual blue eyes, and said, "Oh. I didn't see you come in."

Which made no sense to Ian. Of course she hadn't seen him—she'd been looking at the book. She might have *heard* him come in; seen him, no.

"I will take the babies riding tomorrow," Ian said, sitting down close to her. Her scent, familiar to him now, and so dear, began easing him, and his thoughts cleared. "Come with us." A ride to the folly high on the hill, winter sunshine, his wife and children snuggling at his side . . .

"I'd love to." Beth's face softened. "But I can't, you know. There is so much to do, more guests arriving, the menus to be sorted. Since Chef has left for France, Cook is having hysterics by the hour. She's terrified she won't be able to manage, even with the extra help we've hired." Beth rubbed her temples. "It is becoming quite an ordeal."

Ian sensed her unhappiness, but he relaxed, because he knew exactly how to make her feel better. That was another thing he could do that didn't involve crowds, or understanding how to answer people correctly, or looking into their eyes.

He started to lift the book from Beth's lap, kissing her cheek at the same time. Beth grabbed the book and pulled it back.

"Wait. I wanted to show you." She pointed to a picture, a colored illustration, protected by a leaf of thin paper. "What do you think of this one? It's very like the one I broke, isn't it? Same sort of vines and dragons, but in green and gray, instead of blue. The book says it's owned by a gentleman in France. I could write him."

Ian glanced at the picture, taking in every nuance of the bowl in two seconds flat. How could she think it was like the one the Russian had? Clearly it was not, or Ian would have purchased this bowl in the first place.

But he'd learned, to his amazement, that most people couldn't tell one Ming bowl from the other. The fanatics who shared his passion could, and they were the few human beings with whom Ian could speak at length and understand in return—at least, as long as they remained on the topic of Ming pottery. Hart had explained that a person either had the gift or did not, and Ian needed to show compassion toward those who didn't.

"No," Ian said, trying to soften the word. It sounded harsh all the same, falling flat against the thick velvet drapes at the windows. "It's not the same."

"But look." Beth traced the line of vine with her finger. "Surely the pattern is identical. I checked it against the book in which you found the first one . . ."

Ian lifted the tome away again, and this time, Beth let him. "It isn't blue," he said.

"Well, I know it isn't *exactly* the same, but . . ."

Ian closed the book and carried it to a table, taking a moment to line up its edges exactly with those of the wood. Once he was satisfied that the symmetry was perfect, he returned to the ugly sofa and sank down next to Beth. He sat shoulder to shoulder with her, hip to hip.

"I started collecting the bowls a year and four months after I came home from the asylum," he said.

Beth looked at him to listen, her gaze catching his. Her eyes were such a lovely color, blue with flecks of gold, like sunshine on a pond. Ian got lost in looking at her eyes a moment, forgetting what he'd been saying.

"You began collecting a year or so after you came home . . ." Beth prompted.

Ian's mind picked up the thought and returned to that gear. "I went into an antiques shop with Isabella, in Paris."

Ian stopped again, remembering how terrified he'd been to leave Mac's hired townhouse, how soothing Isabella's presence had been when she'd persuaded him to accompany her. His sister-in-law had known how to speak into Ian's panicked silences, how to calm him with a smile, how to ask his opinion and then give it for him, so that strangers wouldn't think him odder than he was.

He remembered that his brothers had been puzzled and angry that Ian had let Isabella lay a hand on his arm or give him a quick kiss on the cheek, when he refused to let the rest of his family touch him.

Ian had thought his brothers fools about that. If they couldn't understand the difference between three over-bearing Scotsmen who smelled of smoke and whiskey, and a lovely young woman scented with attar of roses, he couldn't help them.

"Ian?"

Ian had lost track again. He looked into Beth's face—the woman who'd saved him from himself and who loved him in spite of his many, many shortcomings—and the words went out of Ian's head. Nothing he'd been saying could be as important.

"Isabella likes to shop, yes," Beth said, watching him expectantly. "And she took you into an antiques shop. Did you see a Ming bowl there?"

Beth always insisted Ian tell the end of a story, no matter that, in his head, he'd finished with the subject and moved on.

"It was beautiful." Ian forced the memories to return. "Translucent white and brilliant blue. The lines were perfect. Chrysanthemums and dragons, a lotus flower on its bottom. I couldn't stop looking at it."

He remembered his younger self standing in the center of the shop, staring at the bowl, riveted in place. Isabella telling him it was time to leave, and Ian refusing to go. His world had been so heavily gray, and the incandescent colors of the bowl had stood out like a beacon of hope.

"Isabella told me not to buy it, but she didn't understand." Ian wanted to laugh at the memory. Isabella had been bewildered, so sure Hart would shout at her for letting Ian spend so much. "I had my own money. Curry wrote out the cheque for me, and I took the bowl home. I was only at ease in my mind when looking at it. So Isabella found another one for me. That one wasn't right, but the next one she showed me was. After that, I looked for them myself."

"Only bowls." Beth smiled the warm smile that had crashed over him like a wave of sunshine the first time he'd seen it. "I remember when you told me that."

Ian looked away and studied the floor about a foot in front of his boot, unable to concentrate with her beauty flooding him. "I like the shape." He didn't buy the bowls for their value, though he knew to the farthing what each was worth. He would completely ignore a perfect specimen that cost a fortune if he didn't like it. "When I saw the one from Russia, I knew it was special."

Beth's fingers curled into her palms. "Ian, you are breaking my heart. I didn't mean to drop it."

Ian, pulled back to her, put his hand on her small ones and looked up into her face. "That bowl was special because of the blue. It exactly matched your eyes."

CHAPTER SEVEN

*B*eth stopped. Her lips parted and a tear dropped to her cheek. "Oh, Ian."

Ian stared at her in surprise, pain touching his heart. He hadn't meant to make her cry. He'd intended to explain why she shouldn't bother trying to replace the bowl for him, so she would stop worrying about it.

As he watched the tears streak her cheeks, old dark anger built inside him, the one that manifested when Ian couldn't understand what he'd done. The angry beast told Ian that he was mad, unworthy of her, and would lose her in the end.

Ian kicked at the darkness, which he hadn't felt in a long time, willing it to recede. He cupped his hands around Beth's face, brushing away her tears.

"Why are you crying?" He felt the desperation rise, the need to understand.

"Because it was special to you. And I ruined it."

Words deserted him. He saw only Beth's tears, her

blue eyes wet. He couldn't find the way to explain, to stop her weeping.

He growled in frustration as he tilted her face to his and kissed her lips.

The touch of her mouth was like a balm, soothing hurt. Ian let himself be lost in the warmth of her mouth, the taste of her breath.

He needed to touch her, to be surrounded by her warmth. He'd take her to bed and kiss away her tears, give her pleasure so deep she'd forget about the confounded bowl.

Ian had learned all about physical pleasure long ago, how to give it, how to enjoy it. He'd had trouble with emotions—with mastering them, or at times, even feeling them. But physical joy he understood. He'd sought it to replace the more profound emotions he knew he'd never experience.

Beth had taught him otherwise. The marriage of the physical with the love she'd awakened had opened an entire world to Ian, one more amazing than he'd ever imagined.

He slid his arms around her, Beth making a noise in her throat as his kisses landed on the exposed skin of her shoulders and breasts.

As he reveled in the taste of her, her scent of cinnamon, sweat, dust, the back of his mind began to work.

Beth liked it when Ian did things for Jamie and Belle. When the children were pleased by his gifts or his attention, Beth laughed, she hugged Ian impulsively, she'd even kiss him in front of people, Beth who was so modest in public.

Ian remembered something he'd discovered acciden-
tally one evening while idling away time waiting for his
brothers. He'd tucked the idea and its beautiful precision
into the recesses of his brain to be examined at another time,
but now he brought it forth. Belle might not understand
beyond the amusement of it, but Jamie would be delighted.
He liked precision almost as much as his father did.

The idea caught at Ian so abruptly that he broke
the kiss.

Beth touched his face. "What is it? What's wrong?"

He decided not to tell her. When he'd surprised Beth
in the past with gifts, her astonishment had increased her
delight, and Beth was at her most beautiful when she
was delighted.

He'd tell no one. Ian couldn't trust Mac, Cam, Hart,
or Daniel not to give away his secrets. He wanted to
keep it special and private for his children, for Beth. The
perfect Christmas gift.

Ian felt a smile spread across his face before he could
stop it. Joy of joys, Beth smiled too, no more tears,
though her lashes were still wet.

Ian kissed her again, and she responded, her mouth
softening for him, hands seeking his body. He unfastened
the intricate buttons of her bodice, then Ian let himself
grow lost in the beauty of her, sorrow forgotten.

A PRUSSIAN PRINCE WAS ONE OF THE HOUSEGUESTS
that year, and he arrived in splendor with his entourage a
few afternoons later. Hart had invited him, first because
the man was a longtime friend, and second, because Hart

was still uneasy about how Germany was building up industry, including arms manufacturing. His princely friend was in the position to know many things, and Hart intended to use his visit to learn those things and pass them on to those who could act on the knowledge.

Hart stood with Prince Georg in the long upstairs gallery, which was filled with paintings of dour Mackenzie ancestors, interspersed with bright land-scapes by Mac or his portraits of Mackenzie dogs past and present. The two men indulged in cigars as they looked out the long windows at the thin layer of pristine snow covering the Mackenzie lands, trees on distant hills outlined in silver.

The conversation had turned to Hart delicately probing for information about an armaments factory, when Beth rushed toward them in a swirl of rust-colored poplin.

"Hart, there you are. I need to speak with you." She passed the two gentlemen but looked back, her eyes wide, when Hart didn't move. "Urgently. I beg your pardon, Your Highness."

Georg smiled—the handsome, blond prince always had an eye for the ladies.

Beth continued walking at a rapid pace toward Hart's private wing. "*Quite* urgently," she said over her shoulder.

Hart let out a breath. "I need to follow her." He laid his cigar into a bowl on a carved Louis XV table. "My apologies."

"Not at all." Georg's smile indicated he knew damn well that Hart had brought him here to mine him for information. "Perhaps I will take a stroll in your lovely garden."

"If you prefer a warmer activity, an early dinner is being laid on in the dining room. I'll return as soon as I'm able."

"Of course." Georg chuckled. "*Les femmes,* eh?" He always used French when speaking about women.

Hart started after Beth down the gallery. His sister-in-law kept a swift pace, and Hart was striding fast by the time he reached the entrance to his wing of the house.

Beth made for Eleanor's bedchamber and walked in without knocking. Hart entered the chamber to see his wife sitting up in bed, a writing desk on the mattress next to her, a sheaf of papers surrounding her. Menus, Hart saw when he approached. And seating plans, and lists, so many lists.

Next year, Hart would rent a cottage in the middle of the Highlands for himself, Eleanor, and their new baby, and spend Christmas and New Year's in glorious privacy. No parties, no weeks of planning, no dining room full of too damned many people.

A futile dream, he knew. The entire staff of Kilmorgan Castle would follow them into the remote Highlands, never believing that Hart and Eleanor could look after themselves. Considering events of the past, they were probably right.

"No change?" Eleanor asked Beth.

Two pairs of blue eyes turned to Hart, one dark blue, Eleanor's cornflower. A double assault.

"Beth." Hart kept his voice gentle. "I have cabinet ministers and the Admiralty waiting for my report on armaments in Prussia."

"Not to worry," Eleanor said, before Beth could

speak. "You rushing off after Beth over some domestic trouble will disarm Prince Georg admirably. He will relax and tell you everything. But I assure you, this is not a trivial matter. Beth came to me at once, which was the sensible thing to do. And, no, this is not about the cold supper for Boxing Day, although of course, I would value your opinion, as always, although . . ."

"Eleanor," Hart said sharply. Sometimes the only way to stop his wife was to talk over her. "Now that you two have brought me here, please let Beth tell me why."

Eleanor blinked. "Well, of course. Do carry on. Beth is frightfully worried about Ian."

"I think I upset him very much when I broke the bowl," Beth said, diving in before Eleanor could speak again. "He seemed all right for a few days, but now he's locked himself into one of the chambers in our wing and refuses to come out. He went in yesterday evening, came to bed very late, and then got up and went right back inside. He's not come out to eat, he'll not let anyone leave him food, he won't unlock the door. Curry says he used to do this sometimes, before I met him."

Alarm rose in Hart. Ian had on occasion locked himself away from his brothers and the world that bewildered him too much. He'd resist all attempts to make him come out, or even speak, although, he'd at least let Curry leave a tray of food outside the door. Even then, he wouldn't open the door until the hall was completely empty.

Hart tried to remain calm, logical. "All the doors in your wing have the same locks now. A key from any other door will open it."

Beth gave him an exasperated look. "This is Ian. He will have thought of that. He's bolted it from the inside."

Hart's alarm threatened to become panic. "Damnation."

"I'm sorry, Hart." Beth's eyes were red-rimmed. "I'm afraid I might have sent him into one of his muddles."

Ian hadn't had a breakdown for a long time. When he'd first come home from the asylum, he often degenerated into panicked tantrums, or he'd spend days without speaking to anyone. His body had been present, but his mind had not. Watching Ian stare straight ahead, refusing to look at Hart or respond to his words, had been heartbreaking.

The incidents had dwindled as Ian grew used to living at home and being around his brothers. They'd all but stopped after he'd met Beth, and they'd ceased altogether after he and Beth had moved into Ian's private house not far from here. The birth of Ian's children had relaxed him still more, a tension Ian had carried for so long easing away.

But Hart had never understood what had made Ian fly into his frustrated rages. Beth might be right, as much as Hart wanted her to be wrong.

Hart went to Eleanor and leaned to give her a brief embrace. She kissed his cheek, her scent and warmth lending him strength.

"Show me where he is," Hart said to Beth. "And send for Ainsley."

CHAPTER EIGHT

*I*an heard the knocking on the door, but as though from far away. He was on his hands and knees behind a desk, working on a tricky bit. His fingers were steady as he set each object into place.

Vectors, momentum, resistance, acceleration, velocity —numbers and equations swam in his head, and he spoke softly to himself as he worked.

"The angle should be *this*, not *this*. *A* not *B*. Damn it."

He dropped one, which could have been a catastrophe, but he knew exactly where to pull another out of line. Still cursing under his breath, he set the pieces in place again.

The knocking turned to banging. "Ian, open the door."

The stentorian tones of Hart came rolling through the wood. Ian paid no attention. Hart liked to tell the world what to do, but Ian had learned long ago how to ignore him.

"Ian." The shout turned to a roar.

Another rapid knock. "Come on, guv. You've got us worried something powerful."

Ian took another piece from the box and set it carefully into its place. Why, when a man wanted to retreat and do something useful, something interesting, did the entire family have to bluster their way in? Ian had learned to follow certain conventions so his brothers wouldn't worry too much about him—leaving a note when he slipped away for a few days to fish, for example, instead of simply disappearing.

Not that Ian was good at explaining or remembering to leave notes, but he'd learned that these things kept his family calm. Ian was a perfectly healthy and strong man, yet Hart could fuss so whenever Ian went for a long walk.

Ian had bolted the door, because if anyone opened it, not only would they ruin the surprise, they'd let the bloody dogs in. *That* would be a disaster.

"Ian!" Hart's voice rose like battering thunder. "Open the door before I have Bellamy fetch an axe."

"Hart," Ian said, raising his voice and speaking carefully so there'd be no misunderstanding. "Go. Away."

"Ainsley," he heard Hart rumble.

"I can hardly pick a lock if there is no lock to pick," came Ainsley's crisp, clear tones. "The bolt's on the inside. You overestimate my skills."

"Then we go for the axe. Mac, get Bellamy."

"Don't you dare bash a hole into Ian's study door," Beth said. Good girl—she'd put Hart in his place. "It will be weeks before we can get a builder at this time of year, and I refuse to live with a door that is so much firewood."

"Persuasion is doing nothing," Hart said, angry. "Even yours."

"Stop it, both of you," Ainsley broke in. "Let me try."

Ian heard the lock of the door click—they'd have found a key for the main lock, which was why he'd had a bolt installed on his private study long ago. When he did mathematics equations that took his entire concentration, he didn't want a maid, footman, or his brothers invading the room and distracting him.

As they were doing now. A faint *scratch, scratch* sounded, Ainsley setting to work.

At least they'd stopped banging. Ian opened another parcel and reflected that he needed more, much more. He'd have to send to Inverness, maybe farther. How long for a package to arrive from Edinburgh or Glasgow—in time for him to finish for Christmas?

The voices outside the door lowered to normal tones, and Ian put them out of his head. When he finished for the day, he'd take Beth and the children for a walk, or show Beth how well they were progressing with riding.

"What are you all doing?" Daniel's voice floated over the others. "Disassembling doors now, are we?"

The others explained rapidly, Ian trying to shut out the voices. Daniel was clever—if anyone could get the door open, it was Ian's quick-witted nephew. Daniel had blossomed in the last year, with lightning-swift thoughts, an ability to think of ten solutions to any problem, and a knack for building strange but useful gadgets. He even talked about heavier-than-air flight, about wind, air mass, and fixed wings. Any machine, from steam to electric to the forays into combustion engines, fascinated Daniel.

"Here, let me try this," Daniel said. Something snicked against the door with a more decisive sound. "I've found it useful prying back bolts on hotel room doors."

"And why, son, were ye prying back bolts on hotel room doors?" Cameron's growl sounded in heavily accented Scots.

Daniel's answer was innocent. "Oh, university high jinks. Pranks. You know."

Ainsley said, "If it involved ladies, do not tell me."

Daniel snorted a laugh. "Very well, stepmama. Ah, I have it."

The bolt slid back and the door handle moved. Ian was already up and leaping across the room, knowing exactly where to put his feet so he wouldn't ruin what he was building.

He reached the door and slammed his hand against it just as Daniel swung it open.

"No," Ian said. "Stay out."

Daniel's head came around the door, Ainsley's fair one below it. "Good heavens, Ian, what are you doing?" Ainsley asked.

"Let me in," Hart said in a harsh voice.

Ian felt the door give, and he shoved back. "Daniel, keep him out. Don't let Beth see."

"Don't let Beth see what?" came Beth's anxious voice.

Hart brought his fists down on the door and shouldered his way past Daniel. He saw the state of the room and stopped. "What the devil?"

Daniel's quick glance took in everything, and his eyes started to sparkle. Hart's brows came down, his anger not abated. "Come out of there, Ian," Hart said. "You're worrying Beth."

"When I'm finished," Ian said.

Hart started to argue, but Daniel stepped into the room and held up his hand. "No, no wait. I think I know what he's doing." He scanned what Ian had set up. "Bloody marvelous."

"What?" Beth asked. "Move, Hart, I want to see."

Daniel whirled, kilt spinning, and spread his arms. "Ian's right. Everyone out, or you'll ruin it. Beth, it's a surprise. You'll like it. I promise."

Hart remained fixed in place. Daniel didn't move, and Ian kept his hand on the door, ready to slam it shut.

"I'll stay and help Ian, Uncle Hart. But you all have to go. And leave him alone. I'll look after him."

Hart's expression was murderous. Ainsley shook her head and withdrew.

"Thank you, Danny." Beth's voice came from the hall, but she remained without and didn't try to push her way in. "Come along, Hart. If Daniel says it's all right, it must be."

"Yes, let's go have some tea," Ainsley said. "Eleanor will be dying to hear what is happening. Besides, don't you need to pry secrets out of a Prussian prince?"

Hart didn't answer either of the ladies. He held Ian's gaze, and Ian didn't let himself look away. He knew that Hart was reassured when Ian looked into Hart's eyes, taking it as a sign that Ian hadn't slipped back into madness. Gazing into Beth's eyes was easy—they were so beautiful; *she* was so beautiful—but Ian still wasn't always comfortable sharing so intimate a glance with anyone else.

But he'd learned that he could look at his brothers if he wanted to. And if it meant they went *away* and left him in peace, so much the better.

Hart at last gave Ian a nod, turned around, and stalked away, as though going had been his idea. Ian heard Beth and Ainsley begin talking at once, Cameron's growl, less edgy than before, and Curry's exasperated exclamation that looking after Ian was putting lines on his face.

Daniel closed the door and beamed a wide smile. "What a setup. For Beth, you say?"

"For Jamie and Belle." Ian liked that Daniel moved carefully, not disturbing what Ian had put into place. "Which will make Beth happy again."

"You're amazing, Uncle Ian. The only man in Scotland who can put an entire house in an uproar by locking a door."

"I didn't want the dogs in."

"Good thinking. Now." Daniel put his hands on his kilt-clad hips. "I have a few gadgets I could add—clockwork figures, clockwork noisemaking machines, and . . . clocks. Will you let me?"

Ian imagined it, the timing, speeds, and events. "Yes," he said.

Another thing Ian liked about Daniel was that he didn't need long explanations and reassurance. He only laughed and rubbed his hands.

"Right," Daniel said. "Let's get to it."

DAVID FLEMING WALKED INTO CASTLE KILMORGAN

and made a rude gesture to the Mackenzie ancestors glaring down from the walls at him. David was connected to these people, as his great-great aunt, Donnag Fleming, had been daft enough to marry a Mackenzie. David was descended from Donnag's brother, and that was as close as he wanted to become to being a Mackenzie.

The quantity of whiskey sloshing around inside him didn't help when looking up at all these people. Nor did the long journey and lack of sleep.

At least Hart had comfortable beds, David thought. He knew he should be at home managing his own estate, but that seemed boringly tedious, and too much like the life his father had wanted him to lead. Hence his eager acceptance of Hart's Christmas invitation.

I'll be a staid lord of the manor when I can't stand up anymore.

There was one drawback about staying in Hart's house, however. When the footman took David's wraps, he informed him that His Grace was waiting for David in a chamber in the duke's private wing.

Ah, well, best to get it over with. David straightened his cravat in front of a mirror on the second landing, brushed back his dark hair, and tried to convince himself that his eyes weren't as bloodshot as they felt.

At least his valet had stuffed him into a new suit. Hart would have him in a kilt for the rest of the visit, but David was happy he'd been able to make the drafty train journey with his legs covered.

He knocked on a door near the end of the corridor as directed by a helpful maid dusting in the hall. Not Hart's bedchamber. However, he knew that Hart had changed his bedchamber after his marriage, declaring he wouldn't sleep in the monument dedicated to his father any longer. Not that David blamed him, but that meant he was being directed to . . .

A maid opened the door from the inside, gave David a deferential smile, then slipped away, carrying out whatever tray she'd come here to remove.

Hart Mackenzie, the Duke of Bloody Kilmorgan, sat on a gilded chair from the last century, ruining its finish by rocking back on the chair's legs and resting his feet on the large bed beside him.

In that bed, like a queen on her throne, reposed Eleanor, Duchess of Kilmorgan, formerly Lady Eleanor Ramsay, the woman with whom David, once upon a time, had fallen madly in love.

Tonight she lay in a modest dressing gown, pillows behind her, covers pulled up under her arms. Nothing could hide the large bulge of her abdomen, the symbol of her love for David's oldest friend, Hart Mackenzie.

CHAPTER NINE

*D*avid." Hart brought his legs down and swung up and out of the chair, sounding genuinely glad to see him. "Welcome."

His handshake was warm and strong, Hart's clap on David's shoulder as hard as ever.

"Forgive me for not rising," Eleanor said, her smile as lovely as he remembered. "For obvious reasons. I had an awful morning, and I was told unequivocally that I needed to rest." She glanced at Hart, who paid no attention. "It's good to see you, David. Come and give me a kiss."

Oh Lord. David pasted on a smile as he crossed the room, took Eleanor's outstretched hands, and leaned down to kiss her cheek. She smelled of honey and lavender, and she was still beautiful, even with, or perhaps because of, her face and hands plump with her pregnancy.

"I'm so glad you've come," Eleanor said softly.

No false politeness. She meant it.

David didn't deceive himself, however. He'd always known he hadn't stood a chance with Eleanor, no matter how besotted he'd become. Eleanor had refused David years ago, after Eleanor and Hart's very public breakup, and she'd never married at all until she had a chance again with Hart. It had always been Hart with her.

"Better than me rotting at home alone at Christmas," David said in a jovial voice. "A Christmas cracker isn't much fun to pull open on your own."

Eleanor winked at him as she released his hands. "There will be plenty of people to break them with here. Especially a few young ladies."

David backed away from the bed and dropped into a chair. Dear God, even the decorative furniture in this room was comfortable.

"No matchmaking, El," David said. "Don't you dare. I'm a drunken sot, and the women who like me are not the sort I'd introduce to my mother. I prefer it that way."

Hart had resumed his chair, observing the exchange in his eagle-eyed way. He didn't hover and growl like a jealous husband, but the watchfulness was there.

Foolish man. Eleanor was madly in love with Hart, the Lord only knew why. Hart had been the very definition of the decadent rake in his younger days, with David his avid disciple, though sometimes his tutor.

"I feel certain there is someone out there for you," Eleanor said. "It's only a matter of narrowing down possibilities and presenting opportunities."

"No," David said emphatically. He hooked his ankle around a footstool and dragged it to him, settling his dirty boots on it. Exhaustion was beating on him, making his eyelids sandy.

"Leave him be, El. He's our guest." Hmm. Was that Hart Mackenzie being so kind and understanding?

"True," Eleanor said. "And there's the matter of the little task we need him to do."

Ah ha. Hart was never kind without a reason.

"So you called me here to work, did you?" David asked. "And all I thought was that I'd take advantage of your soft beds and excellent food."

"And you will," Eleanor said, smiling that smile that meant she was up to something. "We need it done before Christmas Eve, and then you can sit back and feast as much as you wish."

"Good." David's eyes narrowed. "What is this task for which you need my expertise?"

"Blackmail the Earl of Glastonby," Eleanor said.

She spoke in a matter-of-fact voice, as though she commanded her husband's friends to blackmail a gentleman every morning, two after teatime.

"Glastonby?" David's tiredness ebbed as interest took over. "Prudy Preston that was? He was head lad at school," he explained to Eleanor. "Ready to pounce as soon as you even looked as though you thought about breaking a rule. Still that way. What has he done to be blackmailed by *you*, Eleanor?"

"Nothing yet," Hart said quietly.

"Now, this sounds more intriguing." David reached for the flask inside his coat and took a drink of whiskey. "I believe I take your meaning. You wish me to goad Glastonby into a compromising position, and then threaten to tell the world about it, unless he gives me . . . what?"

"A Ming bowl," Hart said.

"A Ming . . . You've lost me."

"For Ian," Eleanor said. She'd placed her hands on her abdomen, and her face took on a faraway expression, a mother lost in the contemplation of her child.

Pain like a poisoned dart stabbed David's heart. He did not so much wish anymore that Eleanor would carry *his* child, but he envied Hart for having a beautiful wife, thick with his firstborn, so in love with her husband that she'd help him ask his friend to do a spot of blackmail for him.

David shifted uncomfortably, wishing the pain would go away. "Ian collects Ming bowls, yes," he said. "And you are saying Glastonby has one. The question I ask myself is, why do you not simply purchase the bowl from Glastonby?"

"He won't sell," Hart said. "I've spent the last week and a half tracking down a bowl almost exactly like one of Ian's that was broken—a blue one. The design has to be blue, Beth says. Glastonby has the closest I can find. I made a large offer for it, which he promptly turned down. Won't sell to a Mackenzie, he said. Not to me, not to Ian, not to any of our wives. We are tainted and don't deserve to possess such beauty."

"Sounds like something Prudy Preston would say."

"Quite vexing of him," Eleanor said. "Ainsley offered to steal it, leaving a substantial payment for it, of course, but Hart's idea is better. You can obtain the bowl for us and put your Prudy Preston in his place at the same time."

She looked so smug, so confident as she plotted Glastonby's doom. The man didn't stand a chance.

David took another sip of whiskey. "Your wife is dangerous, Hart. Do you know that?"

"Aye, so I've learned." Hart's solemn tone made David want to laugh. The great Mackenzie, feared by men and adored by women, had been brought to his knees by blue eyes, a wide smile, and a bloody devious mind.

"And therefore," David said, "you called in the expert on all things perfidious, your old friend, David Fleming."

"You'll do it?" Eleanor asked. "Excellent."

"Of course I will do it. I'd do anything for you, El, and you knew that, which is why you had your servant send me up here. What had you planned to offer me as a reward?"

Eleanor shrugged. "Soft beds, a feast at Christmas and Hogmanay."

"All very tame and domestic. I'll do this, but we'll discuss my price later. That will give me time to think of something outrageous—"

A soft tap on the door cut off David's speech, followed by the door opening, and the creaking Wilfred putting his head around the doorframe. "Your Grace. There is the matter of letters to sign before I depart for Kent." Wilfred's tone was less apologetic than reproachful.

Hart rose at once. Tamed by his wife, tamed by his secretary. Amusing.

David's amusement faded when Hart leaned down and gave Eleanor a kiss. The kiss turned from a brief good-bye to something more passionate, more intimate, more private.

The look Eleanor gave Hart when he lifted away

shattered any illusion David might have harbored that Eleanor ever had been torn between the two men. She looked at Hart with pure love, nothing less.

"Talk to El for a moment," Hart said, following Wilfred. "Don't upset her." The flash in his eyes told David that all the wars of the world would be nothing to Hart's rage were Eleanor to be upset.

David saluted with his free hand. He took another pull of whiskey as Hart closed the door, then tucked the flask back into his pocket.

"How are you, Eleanor? Truly. You can tell Cousin David."

"Truly wonderful. Running such a large household has its difficulties, but we are weathering."

"Even having to run it while you're laid up?" David gazed at her distended belly under the covers. "Once upon a time, I'd hoped that . . ." He gave the unborn Mackenzie a nod. "But it wasn't meant to be, I suppose."

"No, it wasn't. I'm sorry, David, if I ever hurt you."

"Hurt me? You ripped out my heart and kicked it about a mile, but no matter, dear lady. I'm made of resilient stuff." David decided to stop being selfish for two seconds in his life. He let his voice grow gentle. "You're madly in love, El. It shows on you, and it shows well. And it is obvious that Hart is madly in love with you in return. He always has been."

Eleanor's glorious smile spread across her face. "I believe he is, though when I when I was younger, I was too daft to understand that."

"And I have never forgiven Hart for the way he treated you." David got to his feet, alarmed when his legs swayed under him. "He deserves to be thrashed

soundly. Although he paid for his mistakes, I would say."
David leaned his fists on the bed, more to steady himself
than anything else, and leaned down to kiss her cheek. "I
am happy for you, El. And for Hart, the blackguard. I'm
not so much of a bastard that I'd wish you any
unhappiness."

"And you'll always be dear to us, David."

David snorted a laugh as he stood up, or tried to. The
nips from the flask had been a mistake. "Don't grow
sentimental. I'm only *dear* to Hart when he wants something. David does his dirty deeds."

"This one is in a good cause."

"For baby brother Ian? Yes, I suppose it is. And if
you think I loathe to go to the Earl of Glastonby and
threaten dire things, you're wrong. I'm looking forward
to it." He leaned down and kissed Eleanor again, because
what fool wouldn't when he had the chance?

"David." Hart's voice rumbled behind him. "Please
take your hands off my wife."

David carefully straightened up, showing that he
touched Eleanor only in friendship. Well, he didn't want
to, but he'd keep it cordial.

"Leave me alone, you lucky bastard," David said. If
he weren't so drunk and exhausted, he'd be more
restrained, but if he didn't find a bed soon, he was going
to die. He used Hart's arms to steady himself as he
passed him. "If you make her unhappy for a single
second, my friend, I will shoot you."

"My valet is waiting outside to help you. Sleep it off."
Hart patted David on the shoulder.

The pat was friendly, but hard, and David had to
struggle to keep to his feet. David blew a mischievous

kiss to Eleanor, then swayed out the door and happily let
the valet have his way with him.

"THERE, GUV. HOW'S THAT?"

Ian, dressing in the dark morning, paused impatiently. He wanted to fetch his children, meet Cameron
and Gavina for their early ride, and then get back to his
task in the sitting room. Christmas was nearing, and he
and Daniel weren't finished.

Now Curry had turned from the wardrobe in Ian's
dressing room and faced Ian with something resting on
his small palms.

It was a Ming bowl, or what looked like one, but
cracked and crazed with bits missing. Ian stared at it a
moment, then losing interest, went back to buttoning his
riding coat.

"It's your bowl," Curry said. "The one you bought
from the Russian. Me and the others below stairs, we
stuck it back together for you."

Ian looked at the bowl again. He knew full well that
it was the bowl Beth had broken, with its pleasing lines
of dragon and vine, and the lovely blue. When Ian had
first taken it out of the box, it had sung like a symphony.
Now it was broken, like a violin that would never make
music again.

"No need," Ian said. "It's ruined."

Curry lowered his hands, his brows drawing down,
that look on his face that meant Ian had disappointed
him somehow. "You know, working for you can be
bloody painful, my lord."

Ian straightened his collar. So Curry had said before. Ian never had any idea how to respond to that.

"This took us a long time, guv. And some of the bits had been broken to powder, so of course it can't be all there again."

He sounded exasperated. But then, Curry often did. Curry had done so much for Ian, however, one constant in Ian's swirling madness. Curry had cared for Ian when no one else had, when the man could have walked away and let Ian drown in his own confusion.

"Curry," Ian said. "Thank you."

"Oh, praise from me master. Do you want the bowl, or not?"

Ian glanced at it again, but the bowl no longer sang, no longer eased his jangled world. "You keep it."

Curry's eyes widened. "You'd give me a priceless Ming bowl?"

"Not priceless anymore. Or throw it away, as you like. I'll buy you a better present."

Curry looked down at it, an unreadable expression on his face. "I'll keep it if ye don't mind. A souvenir. It reminds me of you, this thing does."

Ian had no idea why that should be, but he nodded, glad the discussion was over.

He pulled on his riding boots and took up his hat, forgetting about Curry and bowls, broken or otherwise, as his thoughts moved forward to spending a delightful hour with his children.

As Christmas neared, the house filled. Beth was

kept so busy she didn't have much time to worry about Ian, but the thoughts were there, niggling at her. Hart had assured her he'd have a new bowl for her to give to Ian by Christmas, and Beth was warmly grateful to him and Eleanor for their efforts.

Ainsley's four brothers, the McBrides, arrived en masse, Ainsley crying out like a girl as she flew down the stairs to fling herself first at one, then the next. Steven McBride, the youngest brother, came in his regimentals, able to obtain only a few weeks' leave. He was twenty-nine, handsome, tanned from foreign suns, and instantly the center of the female guests' attentions.

Next came Sinclair, the tallest of them with a booming, deep voice—the barrister, who lived mostly in London. The Scots Machine, Ainsley had said his fellow barristers called him, for his tenacious grilling of witnesses at the Old Bailey. He rarely failed to get his conviction.

He might be a machine in court, but Sinclair was also a harassed father with two children—Andrew and Catriona—who immediately turned the nursery into a circus, complete with tents and tightrope walking. Nanny Westlock's face had been tight since their arrival.

Elliot McBride, a former soldier who had been kept nearly a year in a terrible prison in India, arrived with his new wife, Juliana, and his daughter. Elliot had scars on his face and kept his hair shorn, but he'd softened somewhat from the last time Beth had seen him. Married life looked well on him.

Patrick was the eldest, fifteen or so years older than the other McBrides. He'd been father to them when they'd lost their parents, raising the three boys and

Ainsley the best he could. Ainsley clung to him for a long time, and then to Patrick's wife, Rona.

Isabella and Beth, by tacit consent, took over a few of Ainsley's tasks to allow Ainsley to spend time with her beloved family. Still more tasks when Eleanor's father, Earl Ramsay, arrived, so that Eleanor could fuss over him.

Ian, despite his avoidance of crowds, seemed to take the filling house in stride. When he wasn't taking his children out for walks or riding with Cameron and Gavina, he spent it closeted in the sitting room with Daniel. He'd occasionally pass a late evening in the billiards room with the McBride brothers. Beth would look in and see Ian and Elliot smoking in silence while Sinclair and Steven did most of the playing and talking. Ian also quietly won much money from the other three.

Daniel was the Mackenzie who gave Beth the most concern. He'd become as obsessed as Ian over whatever they were doing in the sitting room, bolting down the stairs whenever mysterious packages arrived at the door. In fact, while Ian would emerge from the room from time to time, Daniel remained behind. There was no question of unlocking the door and taking a peek on the rare occasion both left the room, because Daniel had sent for parts for a new lock and installed it himself—and he kept the only key.

Three days before Christmas, Beth came upon Daniel and Bellamy facing each other in a dim back corridor. Bellamy and Daniel both had fists raised, and Daniel sported a large and multicolored bruise from his forehead to his jaw.

CHAPTER TEN

*D*aniel! What on earth?"

Bellamy lowered his fists and stepped away from Daniel, his stoic expression in place.

"Oh, hello, Auntie," Daniel said with his usual brisk cheerfulness. "Bellamy's giving me a few lessons in boxing. I need them, as you can see."

"I do see. Bellamy didn't give you *that*, did he?"

Bellamy looked faintly alarmed, but Daniel laughed. "Nae, not Bellamy. Lad down the pub. The barmaid's been me mate for years, but her new intended didn't see it that way."

Barmaid. Beth's maid Katie had related the gossip about what had happened in the village since their last visit. "Ah, yes. She's marrying the blacksmith's boy."

"Aye, biggest lad in town. We went a round or two before he knocked me down. Best boxer I ever faced. I came home and asked Bellamy to show me what I did wrong."

"And what did he do wrong?" Beth asked Bellamy.

"Didn't guard right." Bellamy stepped forward, the servant disappearing, the fighter emerging. He held up his fists, arms slightly bent, knuckles loose. "In fighting like that, if your hands are too close to your face, your opponent can shove your fist right back into your own eye, and then get under your reach while you're trying to decide what happened."

He demonstrated by slowly thrusting his beefy fist at Daniel's upraised one, pushing Daniel's back at him. Then Bellamy followed with his other fist, underneath to Daniel's face, right where the bruise was.

Daniel sighed in resignation. "Fair point. Thank you, Bellamy. Hello, Dad."

Cameron came down the hall like an angry bear, the picture softened somewhat by his daughter riding on his shoulders. Gavina saw Daniel, squealed in delight, and held out her arms.

Daniel caught her as she tried to dive off the taller Cameron, then Daniel swung her around, making her squeal all the more.

"Brawling in the pub?" Cameron felt himself torn between exasperation and worry, and also the pang of realization that his son had grown up. Cameron had been brawling in pubs at sixteen, chasing barmaids, fighting for their favors. Danny had gone from babe in arms to tall university lad so quickly. Gavina would grow as quickly, gone before he knew it.

"Not in the pub," Daniel was saying. "In the yard behind. No one was hurt—only the pride of Daniel Mackenzie."

"I heard," Cameron said, retaining his fatherly growl. "Blacksmith was worried I'd fetch a constable to arrest his son for pounding you. I told him it was no more than you deserved. You leave the local barmaid alone, Danny. Trouble only comes of that. Ye don't piss in your own nest. Beg pardon, Beth."

Beth, used to Mackenzie men forgetting to mitigate their words around the ladies of the family, only nodded.

Daniel swung Gavina up on his shoulder. "I'm mates with Kirsten, that's all. We've known each other from babyhood. I'll go shake hands and make peace, all right?"

Cameron had no doubt that Daniel could restore everyone into admiring him again. He had the knack for making people like him—his mother had had that charm, though hers had hidden a foul nature. Daniel's nature was sunny, thank God. "Leave them alone for a bit. You can be a whirlwind."

Daniel shrugged, not offended. "Fair enough. After Christmas then."

"And learn to fight better," Cameron said. Daniel made friends, yes, but he also tended to defend those who couldn't defend themselves and sometimes got beaten for his troubles. "Here, look."

He faced Bellamy, fists raised. Boxing within the rules was all very well, but street fighting was another matter. At Daniel's age, Cameron had been a formidable bare-fist fighter.

Bellamy, always the professional, raised his hands and defended. "You keep your fists up, not down," Cameron said. "That way when you punch, your arm twists with the forward thrust, giving it that much more momentum."

He brought his fist forward in slow motion, straight

at Bellamy's jaw. Bellamy blocked with his arm, swinging his own fist straight upward, under Cameron's reach.

"And that," Cameron said, dancing back out of the way, "is why defensive moves are sometimes better than offensive. You watch what your opponent does, find his weakness, and then strike."

Cameron spun away from Bellamy's hit, came back, and jabbed his fist behind Bellamy's ear. Bellamy, the experienced fighter, blocked that too, but only just.

Daniel watched, a grin on his face. "I'll think on that, and have Bellamy give me more lessons. But I've had a spectacular idea just now."

Daniel's spectacular ideas sometimes left them all breathless, or furniture broken. "What?" Beth asked, sounding worried. Wise woman.

"A boxing match," Daniel said. "Between Dad and Bellamy. You know, for Boxing Day."

Beth laughed. "Danny, it's not called Boxing Day because of boxing."

"I know that. But it would be a good pun. How about it, Bellamy? Everyone would be allowed to watch — guests, servants, guests of servants. You and Dad could show how a match is really done."

Color stained Bellamy's cheeks, but he didn't answer. He wanted to, Cameron could see that. Bellamy had once been celebrated throughout Britain then chucked out by his trainer when the trainer saw no more use for him. In his last fight, Bellamy was supposed to have taken a fall, thus gaining his trainer and cronies much money, but Bellamy had wanted to go out winning. He had won the bout, to the joy of Bellamy's followers.

The trainer, on the other hand, furious and in debt to

dangerous men, had Bellamy followed home and beaten. They'd have beaten him to death had not Mac and Cameron, who'd been at the match, come upon the fight.

They had sent off the thugs, then Mac had taken Bellamy home and sent for a surgeon to patch him up. Because Bellamy had nowhere to go, and no job any longer, Mac hired him. Bellamy had paid Mac back for that kindness with his loyalty ever since.

Ainsley would like it if Cameron let Bellamy, a reserved and somewhat shy man, shine in front of the others. Ainsley rewarded kindness with a smile, a delighted kiss, a nibble on the ear . . .

"Aye, it might be a treat for all," Cameron said. Cameron could win still more praise from Ainsley if he let Bellamy triumph. Bellamy had become smitten, Curry had said, with the maid called Esme, who'd come to the door looking for charity, and had been hired on by Mrs. Desmond and Isabella to help with the frantic preparations for Christmas. Bellamy would welcome a chance to show off in front of her, and Ainsley would enjoy the fact that Cameron had played matchmaker.

And perhaps Ainsley would retreat from her terrible worry about Gavina, who was, at the moment, tugging Daniel's hair and laughing. Daniel, in spite of his tendency toward trouble, had turned out rather well. Between the three of them, Gavina should be all right.

"Your Uncle Hart might not approve, you know," Beth was saying. "It is his house after all, Danny."

"Oh, that's no trouble." Daniel grinned and waved away his formidable Uncle Hart. "He's busy looking after Aunt Eleanor, and I wasn't going to bother mentioning it to him."

"You'd love it here, Maggie," Sinclair McBride said under his breath. He gazed out of the vast, empty library to the vast, empty garden, dusted now with snow, glittering like diamonds under a brief visit from the sun. "Such beauty. And quiet."

Maggie, whom he'd called Daisy in intimate moments, had been gone from him five years now. And still the pain was as sharp as on the day she'd died.

Outwardly, the Scots Machine rolled on—Basher McBride—the criminals called him. Cool, sticking to facts, proving beyond a doubt that the man or woman in the dock had committed the abominable murder, rape, or battering and deserved to be punished. Juries warmed to him, the family man who wanted to protect his children and theirs from harm.

Not that Sinclair couldn't be kind. A first-time young thief who'd stolen an apple to feed his mother would win the Basher's compassion, and he'd argue for leniency. The juries liked that too, even if the judges did not.

Inwardly, Sinclair ached. His heart had stopped beating when Maggie's had, and he wasn't certain it had ever started again.

She'd have loved the gigantic Mackenzie house, with its horde of splendid rooms and spread of grounds, all made beautiful for Christmas. Maggie had loved Christmas. These days, the only interest in the holiday Sinclair could muster was to slip a chunk of money to his valet and instruct the man to buy all the toys Andrew and Catriona could want.

"Begging your pardon, Mr. McBride."

Sinclair turned reluctantly from the window at Nanny Westlock's interruption. He saw the look on her face and held up his hand to forestall her words. "What have they done now?"

"Started a fire. On a bed. They might have taken down the entire nursery."

Sinclair smothered a sigh. Andrew, no doubt. Catriona would have watched the mayhem with her usual quiet detachment. Andrew wouldn't have meant to start the fire. He wasn't an evil lad, just mischievous, reckless, and too curious for his own good.

"My apologies, Miss Westlock. I'll speak to Andrew."

"I have already dealt with the matter, sir." By the pinching of her lips, Andrew must have fought long and hard against being dealt with. "But I must recommend that these children be taken in hand."

Well, of course. And if Sinclair had been capable of taking them in hand, he already would have. "Again, I apologize for Andrew's behavior," Sinclair said. "My wife took care of these things, you see."

Maggie, with her laughter, the Irish lilt to her voice — every "T" a precise stop with her lovely tongue behind her teeth, had been able to do anything with her children. She'd been so beautiful, black Irish, she was called, with dark hair and dark lashes framing deep blue eyes. Catriona had her coloring, while Andrew was pure blond Scots, like his father.

"A good nanny can do wonders, sir. I gather your children have no nanny at all?"

"Not at present," Sinclair answered. "Each one I hire never lasts more than a day. Perhaps you could recommend someone, as capable as your good self?"

Miss Westlock's lips thinned. "I will send you a list, sir. I will also suggest that they are growing old enough to need a competent governess, especially your daughter."

Sinclair acknowledged this with a nod. Andrew would be sent off to school in due time, but Catriona . . . Sinclair wanted her home.

"Thank you, Miss Westlock."

Miss Westlock, with the air of a woman having done her duty, closed the door and withdrew.

Sinclair turned to the window. "Maggie, love," he said softly. "You always told me to have faith, but I'm lost."

Silence met him. The coal fire on the hearth made little noise, and wind blew outside, bringing back the clouds, but the thick panes kept out the sound.

Sinclair sighed, one of his black moods descending and bringing a headache with it. "Talking to you does make me feel better, Daisy. But I *wish* for once, you'd answer me."

"LOUISA!" CAME A DELIGHTED CRY.

Lady Louisa Scranton looked up the stairs, a smile spreading across her face as her exuberant sister Isabella ran down to her. In a moment, Isabella was folding Louisa into her arms. Louisa returned the embrace, soaking up the warmth and fragrance of her sister. Her *happy* sister.

"So good to see you, Izzy."

"Mama." Isabella left Louisa to gather up the woman

in black bombazine, who'd come in behind Louisa. "How are you?" Isabella kissed the dowager countess' cheek. "How was the journey?"

"If you must know, darling, long and somewhat tedious." Their mother returned the kiss. "But all the better for seeing you."

Isabella relinquished her to the care of several servants—the dowager countess loved to be looked after by servants—then Isabella linked arms with Louisa to walk her upstairs to the bedchamber prepared for her.

Isabella chattered breezily about the house, the holiday preparations, about what a wonderful time they would all have. Louisa made the requisite responses, wishing she could let Isabella's joy raise her spirits. But Louisa recently had assessed her life, her mother's life, and their future, and had made her decision.

As Isabella went on in exuberance, Louisa glanced about at the hanging decorations that went all the way up the marvelous staircase, the greenery and streamers warming the cold marble and paneling. She looked down over the railings to admire the giant vase of yellow mums placed on the table on the ground floor.

A man in black strode into the open hall below. A Mackenzie, Louisa thought, then her chest constricted, and her mouth went dry.

He was a Mackenzie, and he wasn't. Lloyd Fellows, the detective inspector, was very like Hart Mackenzie when viewed from afar, with the same commanding air, tall body, and dark hair brushed with red when the light was right. He also had hazel eyes that missed nothing, a sharp face, and a biting wit.

The last time Louisa had seen Mr. Fellows had been

at Hart and Eleanor's wedding, when she'd brazenly kissed him.

Louisa remembered the firmness of his lips, the scent of cigar that clung to his clothes, the taste of whiskey and spice in his mouth. A strong man, capable, unafraid of work and hardship, but his hand had shaken a little as he'd brushed back Louisa's hair.

As though he felt Louisa's gaze on him, Fellows looked up, through the greenery and the railings, and their gazes locked.

Louisa's face flooded with heat, but she would not let herself look away. Yes, she had kissed him. She'd been filled with the joy of the wedding, even with its complications, and a sadness that she'd likely never have such a wedding herself. She'd found this handsome man, as sad and alone as she was, and she'd wanted his warmth.

Fellows halted, his face still, his only acknowledgment of her a faint nod. Louisa tried to nod back, but her neck was too stiff to bend. She and Isabella reached the landing on the second floor, Isabella pulled her around a corner, and Mr. Fellows was lost to sight.

"Here we are," Isabella said, ushering Louisa into a large, sumptuous bedchamber. It was a huge room, larger even than her chamber had been when Louisa had lived in the main house on her father's estate. Her bedroom in the dower house was quite small, a corner room under the eaves.

"It's enchanting," Louisa said. "Izzy, I need to tell you. I've decided something."

Isabella turned around, saw Louisa's face, and quietly told the upstairs maid who was unpacking Louisa's cases to leave them and return later. The maid curtseyed and retreated, though she gave Louisa a curious Scots stare before she left.

Isabella took Louisa's hands. "What is it, darling?"

Louisa took a moment to reflect how beautiful her beloved sister had become. Isabella's hair was a rich red, her eyes the perfect green in contrast, her skin pale but not the chalk white of too delicate a complexion.

Isabella knew how to dress well, her green gown with black piping neither too matronly nor too frivolous, her bustle a manageable size in an age where they all must wear the equivalent of kitchen shelves on the backs of their gowns. Tasteful, elegant, lovely. The stark unhappiness had gone from Isabella's eyes, to be replaced by the contentment of a woman who was well loved.

"I've decided I need to get married," Louisa said.

Isabella squeezed Louisa's hands and started to smile, then the smile faded. "I was about to ask who was the lucky gentleman, but suddenly I'm not sure what you mean."

"I mean that it is time for me to marry. I've been of marriageable age for years now, and am actually already on the shelf. I am regarded with pity, despite the fact that I'm an earl's daughter, because papa died in disgrace and poverty. I'm not much of a prospect, am I? But there are men of fortune willing to seek a pedigree, and I do at least have that."

"Darling, you don't need a fortune. Mac and I will take care of you and Mama, you know that. You never have to worry."

"Yes, and you both are very kind." Louisa withdrew her hands from her sister's grasp. "But I *want* to marry. I want my own household, children. I do not wish to be the spinster sister living on charity the rest of my life. If I marry well, not only will you have me off your hands, I can help restore the reputation of the Scrantons, which is a bit damaged, you must admit. I can hear the gossips now, if I do this—*Her father died in terrible debt, her sister's scandalous elopement was played out in the newspapers, but at least the younger sister married into a good family.*"

"Louisa." Isabella dropped her distressed look and spoke gently. "I love you dearly. I do understand—you want your dignity back. But please, I beg of you, do not marry against your heart. I would be pleased beyond belief to see you settled and filling your nursery, but only if you're in love. I've witnessed many a loveless marriage, and both parties live in misery, believe me. I followed my heart, as much trouble as it caused, and found true happiness. I have a wonderful husband who adores me, and I love him and my three children with every breath."

Yes, she did. Mac was besotted with Isabella, and she with him. But Isabella's happiness had been a long time in the making.

"That's all very well," Louisa said impatiently. "But when you ran off with Mac, it was a complete mess, and you know it. I don't wish to be unkind, Izzy, but as I observed before, you made things rather difficult for those of us left behind. You followed your heart, but you spent many unhappy years before you and Mac sorted it all out."

"I know." The flash of pain in Isabella's eyes told Louisa just how unhappy those years had been. "But life is a complicated thing. Not easily put right with this marriage or that—a man of fortune, a woman of lineage.

The newspapers will like it if you make such a match, but you won't."

"What choice do I have?" Louisa swung to her cases and started lifting out gowns—Isabella had purchased every one of them for her. "I am the poor relation, I am left off invitation lists because I've been out several seasons now, and no one has shown interest in marrying me. I want to change that. This spring, I will set out to find a husband. I will have to borrow money from you for a new wardrobe, but I will pay you back when I can."

Isabella's competent hands lifted a skirt and shook it out. "What absolute nonsense. Of course, you shall have your wardrobe, and the most glorious Season any young lady could wish. The debs will be green with envy. If you want a husband, you shall have one."

Louisa recognized the determination in her sister, a determination that could flatten forests. "Please do not match-make for me, Isabella. I know the eligible gentlemen in London and the chances I have with each. I've made it my study. I will do this on my own." She let out her breath, softening. "Though I do appreciate your help, Iz. You know that. And Mama will certainly enjoy herself. She adores going out, and she will accompany me everywhere."

"As will I, when I can," Isabella said. "You know that London during the Season is my territory, and I'll be presenting another artist and new violinist at my little gatherings. You shall of course be there to hostess with me."

"As your unmarried sister."

"As my brilliant little sister who would make any

gentleman invited to my house a good wife. Not to worry, Louisa. This will all turn out well."

Louisa let Isabella dream and scheme as they turned to unpacking. Louisa would curb Isabella's enthusiasm when the time came, but for now, she could allow Isabella her enjoyment.

Louisa's treacherous thoughts returned to Mr. Fellows, and the glitter of his Mackenzie eyes as he looked at her across the empty space in the staircase hall.

Mr. Fellows, a working-class man with scandalous connections and illegitimate birth, was a most *in*eligible bachelor. But he kissed like fire, and he'd stirred a longing in Louisa's heart she'd never forgotten.

CHRISTMAS EVE ARRIVED, AND WITH IT, DAVID, BUT without the precious Ming bowl.

"Don't growl at me, Hart," David said, when he reported in. "Glastonby's a tough nut, and I'm cracking him. But it takes time."

CHAPTER ELEVEN

"What am I to tell Beth?" Hart did not want to explain to her that his idea of sending David to coerce the bowl out of Glastonby had failed.

David shrugged. "Tell her that I am working hard and nearing the goal. But Glastonby has become the consummate family man for Christmas, so I thought I'd return to Scotland and enjoy mine."

Hart poured whiskey into cut-crystal glasses and handed one to David, reflecting that David always looked better when he had his teeth sunk into something. His eyes lost their red-rimmed, bloodshot appearance, his puffy face returned to lean lines, and his voice was steady and whole. Hart kept the amount of whiskey in the glass small, and noticed that David sipped it rather than downed it in a single swallow.

"I'll leave after Boxing Day and return with the bowl before New Year's. Promise. Beth can give it to Ian as a Hogmanay present." David broke into a grin. "Believe it or not, you'll owe some of my success to a vicar."

Hart selected two cigars from his humidor and handed one to David. "How so?"

"Ah, thank you." David lit the cigar with a match and spent a moment sucking in smoke. "You know, I maintain my friendship with you because you always stock the finest. The vicar's an old friend—well, old family friend. He's always kept an eye out for me, sort of a substitute father, because mine was rubbish, as was yours. Anyway, he knows Glastonby, agreed that the man was a hypocrite, and said he'd help me, as long as Glastonby's wife and daughters never find out and aren't hurt by it. Glastonby deserves to be shamed, not his family, and I agree. The man insists on keeping me to the straight and narrow."

Hart took a pull of the cigar and chased it with a sip of whiskey. He savored the combination, as he always did, finding enjoyment in every corner of life he could. He'd learned to do so at an early age. "If it works. I need that bowl."

"Oh, it will work, my friend. But for now." David sank into an armchair and stretched out his long legs. "I'll drown in decadence for the next two days, then return to work."

"By New Year's," Hart said in a firm voice. David was loyal, but too easily distracted.

"By New Year's." David saluted Hart with the glass, then gave up moderation and poured the whiskey down his throat.

MAC HAD ESTABLISHED, THE FIRST CHRISTMAS

Kilmorgan Castle had seen the new brood of Mackenzie children, that the family spent Christmas morning in the nursery giving gifts to the children, before the adults partook of the more formal dinner with guests downstairs. Hogmanay would be only family and very Scottish, with bonfires, Black Bun, more presents, the First Footer, another feast, and much celebration.

Beth loved the traditions. Christmas Day during her childhood had been the same as any other, except in the workhouse, when they'd heard a sermon and had a small second helping of bread. New Year's had come and gone without much acknowledgment.

She'd never experienced childish joy at beholding armfuls of gifts carried in by the men of the family, a Christmas tree heavy with decorations made by the ladies and children and laced with popcorn garlands, or the crackers that banged when pulled open to reveal little toys inside. Soon the children were buried in tissue and ribbons, the adults and Daniel helping them open the gifts. The only two of the family missing were Hart, who hadn't yet arrived, and Eleanor, who was keeping to her bed to rest, planning to join the feast at dinner.

The McBride children were included in the festivities this year. Andrew whooped as he dashed about with a stick hobbyhorse that had a real mane. Catriona sat quietly with the large doll that never left her side, contemplating a doll-sized silk tea gown, exquisitely made in the latest fashion. The dress had been crafted by a dressmaker and had been as perfectly wrought as any gown for a lady. Ainsley explained that Sinclair had one made every year for Catriona's doll.

"How lovely," Beth said, sitting down beside Cat. "Shall we dress Dolly in it?"

"Her name is Daisy," Catriona said, with the scorn only a nine-year-old could muster. "Like my mama. And she doesn't want to wear the dress right now."

"Well, that's all right." Beth addressed the doll. "It truly is beautiful, Daisy. Such fine workmanship. A lovely gift."

"Maybe later," Cat said. She hugged Daisy close, burying her face in the doll's golden hair.

Sinclair shook his head as Beth rose. "I give her a gown every year," he said in a low voice. "Cat tells me the doll likes it but prefers not to wear it. Her mother gave her the doll, you see, the Christmas before she passed. So I don't insist."

Beth understood. The last thing Cat's mother had given her would be precious, not to be touched. Beth's mother had given her a hair ribbon a month before she'd passed, for which she'd saved up her wages. Beth had kept it safely wrapped in paper ever after. She still had it.

She didn't miss the flash of pain in Sinclair's eyes. The death of Mrs. McBride had cut this family deeply.

Ian sat a little apart from the children, watching them laugh and squeal as they pulled tissue from their gifts. None of the boxes to Jamie and Belle had come from him, though Beth had assured them that the new scarves, hats, gloves, tin soldiers, and dolls had come from both Mama and Papa.

Ian only sat, arms on knees, and watched. As Beth started for him, one of the footmen flung open the door to admit Hart, who strode in like a king, his arms loaded with boxes. The six Mackenzie children and Andrew

McBride swarmed him, and even Catriona looked up in interest.

"One at a time," Hart roared. The children paid no attention. They grabbed on to his coat or hem of his kilt, and half followed, half dragged him into the room.

Hart deposited the boxes onto a large table, sank into an empty chair much too small for him, and lifted the three smallest Mackenzies—Gavina, Robert, and Belle—to his lap. The others gathered around, talking at once, reaching for the boxes. Hart's visit to the nursery was always An Event.

Ainsley, Beth, and Isabella distributed the gifts, while the other gentlemen retired with Daniel to the side of the room and made what they supposed were sotto voce remarks.

"He looks like a papa bear with all his cubs, doesn't he?" Mac asked.

"A dancing bear," Cameron said.

"They like him," Ian said. "He's kind. He pretends not to be."

"He pretends very well," Daniel said, grinning.

"Yes," Ian answered.

Hart completely ignored them. He helped small fingers undo the parcels, listened to *oohs* and *aahs* at the extravagant toys, many made by the best toy makers in Germany, Switzerland, and France.

"Where's Aunt Eleanor?" Jamie asked.

"Resting," Hart said. "If you are good—and quiet—you can go see her later. She has to stay in bed right now."

"We're always quiet, Uncle Hart," Andrew shouted. "Cat's quieter than me."

"We know, Andrew." Hart gave him a severe look, which he softened as he handed the boy a package. "Something for you."

Aimee held out a paper hat to him. "You have to wear the crown, Uncle Hart," she said. "You're the king of the castle. Next year, your little baby will be the prince or princess."

Hart took the hat with solemn thanks, unfolded it, and put it on his head. His brothers guffawed in the corner.

"Suits you, Uncle Hart," Daniel called. "Truly."

Hart again ignored them, giving his full attention to the children. Beth however, had seen his flash of fear when Aimee had mentioned the baby.

The man was terrified. He feared losing Eleanor and the new child in the same way he'd lost his first wife and infant son. From the dark smudges under his eyes, Hart hadn't been sleeping. Beth would go to Eleanor after the children were finished opening gifts and look after her, to try to give Hart some relief.

Ian stood up abruptly. "Jamie," he said. "Come with me."

Jamie immediately set down the windup soldier Hart had given him, jumping over the empty boxes and crush of tissue and ribbon. Belle slid from Hart's lap, toddling determinedly after her brother.

"Now?" Daniel asked.

"Now," Ian said.

Daniel gave a whoop to rival Andrew's and raced out of the room ahead of Ian. Ian scooped up Belle and handed her to Beth before he leaned down and lifted his two-year-old son.

Saying nothing, Ian followed Daniel out the door, Beth behind him. Hart, eclipsed, growled for the children to not leave the room like a stampede of elephants.

Daniel led them down the stairs and around to Ian's wing, then back up to the sitting room in which Daniel and Ian had spent so much time.

"Wait," Ian said sternly.

Daniel stopped at the door, turning so his back was against it, his hand on the door handle. "Don't worry. I know how this is done."

"Jamie gets to start it."

"Yes, I know. We've talked about it a hundred times."

Ian kept his frown in place. He might plan something over and over, but when the time came for the execution, he'd meticulously make certain that every step was carried out in exact order. He drove everyone mad in the process, but his plans usually worked.

"Do hurry, Ian," Beth said. "I'm on tenterhooks."

"You do have us all a bit curious," Ainsley said, her daughter in her arms.

Ian gave Daniel a nod. "Open the door."

Daniel pulled a key from his pocket, turned it in the lock, and very slowly swung open the door. Beth took a step forward, but both Ian and Daniel moved to block her path.

"Careful, Aunt Beth. One puff of air can set it off."

"Set *what* off? What have you two been doing?"

"Move," Ian said to Daniel.

Daniel stepped aside, and Ian carried Jamie inside. Jamie looked around in awe, then started to laugh. Beth pushed to the doorway, feeling the others press behind her.

She finally saw what was inside the room and stopped in astonishment. "Ian, what on earth?"

Ian set Jamie carefully on his feet. "The other children can come in, but they must stay near the door."

They'd already bustled forward. Andrew was stopped from darting inside and ruining everything by the strong hands of his father and Cameron.

"Jamie," Ian said. "Touch the first one just there."

Jamie, wide-eyed, put his finger on the very first domino, and gently pushed.

The room was covered with the things. Rows upon rows of black and white dominos stood upright on end, spaced evenly apart. They were on the floor, the furniture, window ledges, chair rail, every space a domino could be set. They were interspersed with other things Beth couldn't identify, but dominos were prevalent.

She saw this all in a split second, and then wonder took over.

The first domino knocked against the next, sending it into the next and so on. The momentum of falling dominos became a stream, and then a pattern that swirled around and around the floor.

The line climbed up a little ramp to run across the desk and down a set of books piled like stair steps on the other side. Back to the floor to divide into two patterns, each exactly mirroring the other, resembling the carefully trimmed hedges in the garden below.

Next, the dominos ran up to the window ledge and a colorful box there. A domino hit a lever before the next ones ran around the sill, and out popped a jack-in-the-box. Belle laughed and clapped her hands.

The domino stream ran across a ledge and up onto

the next windowsill. Again one hit a lever, and out of this box popped a clockwork elephant that lifted its trunk and trumpeted before it sank back into the box.

The adults watched, as entranced as the children, as the line of dominos sped back to the floor. It ran in more patterns, then split again. One domino in the second pattern tripped a switch, shooting a toy train out from the shadows on its track. The train whistled and blew real smoke as it raced around to the end of its run, incidentally knocking down the next domino in the chain.

This stream broke into three, each heading a different direction. One stream zoomed across the floor straight at Jamie before veering aside at the last second. Another whirled into curlicues, like flower petals opening on the floor. The third went up a series of ramps, to clatter across the picture rail under the cornice.

The last domino on the rail fell to land against another on the window seat. This stream ran to another box that sprang open in an explosion of sulfur-smelling smoke.

"That's Danny," Cameron said, sounding as delighted as the children. "He's always loved blowing things up."

Another crack and puff answered the remark as the dominos swarmed down the window seat. The next device they triggered released a string of puppets dancing on a wire, a music box below them playing a merry tune. The dominos ran on, tripping a lever on a clock they ran past. The clock chimed, and from its top issued a line of figures that bowed, danced, or tapped drums in front of them, before they disappeared back into the clock.

"Glockenspiel," Daniel said to Jamie's wide-eyed stare. "Friend and I made it."

The stream now met up with the two others that had been flashing around the room. The dominos ran side by side, three abreast, then knocked into others that grew the stream into four and five, then six and seven across. The dominos parted and flowed into a diamond-patterned design, meeting precisely at the end, the streams dissolving back into three before picking up again for the next diamond.

The diamonds finished, reduced the dominos to two streams again, then one, which zigzagged up ramps to the ceiling fixture, its facets removed. The dominos raced around the rim then fell like a waterfall into a pile below. One knocked into the next row, which tripped another box.

Out popped a clockwork bird, which took wing and flapped around the room. Dominos gathered into a wild swirl, tripping more and more, until they all fell down in the middle of the circle.

A final lever tripped, and a box burst open with a puff of smoke and a ball of glittering paper, which exploded over the room.

Confetti rained down in a gentle shower, the last domino fell, and all was silence.

Mac let out a wild whoop, startling Beth out of her stunned stillness. She had to open and close her mouth a few times, her voice not working, as the others bathed Ian in wild applause.

"Ian, you did all this?" Mac asked.

"Daniel put in the clockworks," Ian said quietly, lifting the first domino to stand it upright again.

"It was all Uncle Ian's idea," Daniel said. "Born in that mathematical brain of his. He came up with the designs and how to make them work. I just put together the clockworks. Uncle Ian's a bloody genius."

Ian said nothing. He showed Jamie how to set up the dominos again. Jamie let him get to five before he knocked them down and shouted happily.

The rest of the family swarmed in, adults and children alike, examining the fallen dominos and Danny's devices, exclaiming in excitement. Hart had pulled off his paper crown, but he bent over the patterns as eagerly.

"You'll have to set them all up again," Hart said. "I want Eleanor to see this."

"Uncle," Daniel said in dismay. "It took us weeks to do this lot."

"Take more weeks," Hart said, without sympathy. "Not Eleanor's fault she's abed. She'll want to see it when she's better."

"True." Daniel brightened, with his usual lightning-swift change of mood. "Auntie El shouldn't miss it. Here, Jamie, help me with these."

He led Jamie to another stream, and Ian rose and came to Beth.

"Daniel's right," Beth said to him. "You are a bloody genius. And here I was afraid . . ."

Ian gave her a puzzled look. "Afraid of what? It was for Jamie. For Christmas."

Beth flung her arms around her husband and pulled his tall body down to her. "Ian, I love you so very much."

Ian's strong arms came around her, his warmth filling his embrace. "I love you, my Beth," he whispered against her hair. "Are you happy?"

"Of course I am. It was a fine thing to do. Something only you would think of."

Ian raised his head to give her a long kiss, then he buried his face in her neck, his arms tightening on her back. "Everything's all right then," he said.

"My love, you will not believe what Ian did."

Hart stretched out on the bed next to Eleanor, his eyes sparkling, though his face was too pale. He needed sleep.

Eleanor listened while Hart described the dominos Ian and Daniel had set up. She laughed, even though laughter brought a twinge of pain. "They needn't bother with it again. It must have been much labor."

"Yes, they do need to bother. It will be a nice treat for you after all this. You deserve it."

Eleanor didn't argue. When Hart wanted to bully someone, especially about something concerning her, little could stop him.

"Well, I'm glad Ian did something so good for the children. And all of you, if I read the excitement in your voice right. It makes me feel light, which will be good for when I go down to supper."

"El." The smile left Hart's face, and he became the worried husband again. The *over*-worried husband. "No one will think less of you if you stay and rest. They know the baby is coming soon."

Eleanor sighed. "Sometimes I think he's not coming at all. I wake in the morning, so sure it will be today, and go to sleep as heavy as ever. Stubborn little chap. So like a Mackenzie."

"It's Christmas. Perhaps it will be today."

Hart could be optimistic, but then *he* wasn't lying here like a bloated balloon.

Hart drew a small packet from his pocket and laid it on the covers over her bosom. "Merry Christmas, love."

Eleanor touched the package in surprise. "What's this? I thought you were too Scottish to give presents any time but New Year's."

"I didn't want to wait."

He spoke calmly, almost offhand, but Eleanor heard the need in him, and the fear. He wanted to make certain she received the gift, in case something happened.

Poor Hart. Eleanor tried to reassure him that she was not fragile and frail like his first wife, but he was too aware of the danger. Eleanor was aware of it too, but they could only wait and see what happened.

She unwrapped the tissue around the gift, revealing another wrapping of silk. She opened this as well then gazed in rapture at the earrings that lay on the blue fabric. Soft gold geometric shapes studded with blue stones hung from wires so fine a breath might displace them.

"Oh, Hart." Eleanor lifted one earring, her eyes wide. "This is astonishing." The gold was so thin it could have been paper, but heavy enough to have substance.

"They're from Egypt." Hart slid closer and rested his head on her shoulder. He touched the dangling gold. "An Egyptian queen wore these."

"Truly?" Her fascination increased. "How old are they?"

"Ancient. Made several thousand years before Christ was born."

"They're beautiful. But where did you get them? Did you slip off to Egypt sometime when I wasn't looking?"

"I intercepted them on their way to the British Museum."

Eleanor very carefully lowered the earring. "Then perhaps we should let them be displayed in the museum."

"Rot that. They were destined for a box in a basement, probably to be buried for eternity. I persuaded them to let me have charge of them."

Hart's persuasion could be aggressive. "I see. Then please tell the gentlemen at the museum I will take very good care of them."

"They know."

Eleanor slipped one into her earlobe, then smiled at Hart. "There. Shall I wear them to supper?"

Hart slid his arm behind her, turning her to face him. His lips met hers in a slow, savoring kiss, his finger stealing to the earring and then drawing down her neck, tracing fire.

It would be a while, Eleanor reflected, sinking into his embrace, before they thought of going down to supper.

LLOYD FELLOWS STILL HADN'T BECOME COMFORTABLE with his welcome into the Mackenzie family. Years of animosity, on both sides, took time to fade.

The women of the household—those ladies mad enough to marry Mackenzies—always greeted Fellows

warmly. He had to admit that visits to the duke's grand
mansion were made easier by the soft embraces and
friendly kisses of the four ladies. The gentlemen still eyed
him askance, although Ian, of all people, accepted
Fellows without rancor.

Even so, sitting at the long table in the grand dining
room, amidst Hart Mackenzie's highborn guests, was
unnerving. Those not of the family stared at him in open
curiosity. They were amazed by the fact that the lofty
Mackenzies had not only acknowledged Fellows's birth,
but accepted him as equal to the Mackenzie brothers.
Fellows was a lowly policeman, raised in the slums of
London. He ought to be taking his dinner below stairs.
And yet he sat at the high table, next to the duchess
herself, who'd risen from her bed to preside over
the meal.

More unnerving to Fellows than the guests' glances
and whispers, however, was the presence of Lady Louisa
Scranton, sister to Lady Isabella, seated right next
to him.

CHAPTER TWELVE

*E*xcept for the glance they'd exchanged over the stair railings a few days ago, Fellows had not seen Lady Louisa since his arrival. He'd thought himself safe from any awkward meeting with her until this afternoon, when he'd entered the dining room to find that she'd been seated at his side.

Louisa smiled at him, utterly composed, as though they'd not met on top of a stepladder in this very house last April, as though she hadn't leaned forward and kissed his lips. And then told him she'd contemplated doing so for some time.

Today Louisa was like a bright angel, dressed in bottle green, with a plaid ribbon pinned to her bodice to indicate her honorary connection with the Mackenzie clan. Her red-gold hair had been drawn up into complicated curls on top of her head, with delicate wisps brushing her forehead. Tiny diamonds dangled from her earlobes, and a silver pendant rested on her chest.

She was younger than Fellows, from an aristocratic

family, lovely and graceful, her manners polished. Though her father had lost every bit of capital he'd had, and more he'd never owned, in Louisa's world birth and breeding counted for more than money. She was so far superior to Fellows that she might as well be soaring like a lofty kite while he stumbled along the ground, too slow to follow.

Louisa was perfectly polite to him all through the meal. No indication that she remembered their kiss— their fiery, hot, magical kiss. Her fascination with him, and the kiss, had probably been a whim, long forgotten. If the incident embarrassed her, she made no sign.

After the meal was over and cleared, a grand procession entered the dining room. The butler led it proudly, carrying a masterpiece of a plum pudding, flaming with brandy, the lights lowered to highlight the effect.

Fellows could hear his mother's Cockney voice now —" What's the point of lighting food on fire? Food's too precious to waste making it into a piece of art. It's for eating, innit?"

His mother was at her sister's as usual, enjoying her Christmas meal with her nieces, nephews, and now grandnieces and grandnephews. When Eleanor's letter with the invitation to her first Christmas dinner as Duchess of Kilmorgan had arrived, Mrs. Fellows had bid him go. "It's where you ought to be," she'd said. "You're as good as any duke. You go and show 'em."

Fellows, listening to the others exclaim over the plum pudding, thought he'd be better off at his aunt's house, bouncing his cousins' children on his knees.

A slab of pudding, studded with fruit and smelling of

spices, landed on his plate. Fellows nodded his thanks to the footman who'd served it.

"Careful," Louisa said as Fellows scooped a chunk of cake onto his fork. "You might have a sixpence."

Fellows did enjoy the English tradition of coins or little trinkets stirred into the Christmas pudding, at least he had when he was younger. His aunt usually put in farthings or tiny toys for the children, but he'd always imagined the Mackenzies put in gold guineas.

If they did, none had ended up in his share of the pudding. He tasted treacle, raisins, nuts, cloves, and brandy, plus the creamy rum flavor of the hard sauce, but no silver or gold. Louisa ate in dainty bites, including Fellows in her conversation or joining in with others near her. These guests were more aristocrats Hart wanted to keep well tamed in case he wanted to use them again. Louisa was very good at putting people at ease, he saw, as was Eleanor, who chatted amicably from the foot of the table, her pregnancy well hidden beneath her dress and the tablecloth.

"Oh," Louisa exclaimed, then she smiled as she removed a silver bit from her spoon. "I've found a sixpence."

"Excellent," Eleanor said. She'd barely eaten any of the pudding, but she'd torn it apart to see whether she'd received any coins. "You'll have good luck all the year, my dear."

The sixpence also meant prosperity, Fellows knew, though he assumed the duchess was being delicate in not implying that Louisa needed assurances of money.

Louisa cleaned the sixpence on her napkin then her smile deepened as she held the coin out to Fellows. "You take it, Inspector. It was on the edge of my piece, so it likely was very nearly in yours."

Fellows eyed the glinting silver, then Louisa. "No, indeed," he said. "It was in your slice. I'd hardly take a sixpence away from a lady."

"It's for luck." Louisa still smiled, but her eyes were watchful. "And a memento of the occasion."

Something to remember her by. Yes, he wanted that. And she wanted it. Perhaps. Or she might be teasing him. Fellows had no idea, and his swiftly beating heart didn't care.

It would be ungracious to refuse a gift from a lady. Fellows bowed, held out his hand, and let her drop the sixpence into it. He noted that she was very careful not to touch him.

Those around them watched the exchange, puzzled and curious but too polite to ask. They did, however, begin to speculate on the things sixpence could buy, things even an inspector of Scotland Yard could afford, they said without actually saying that.

It didn't matter. Louisa smiled at him, all he needed to make him forget silly games with pudding and thinly veiled insults. Let them fire at him. Louisa's smile took all the sting away.

~

"Mac, I can't see where I'm going if your hands are over my eyes."

"Almost there." Mac was warm behind her, his fingers gentle on Isabella's face.

"We ought to be downstairs," she said. "The ball's about to start."

"True, but this has been the only time all day I've been able to bring you up here." Mac led her into the room, and Isabella heard him kick the door closed behind them. "You may look now."

Mac slid his hands from Isabella's eyes and turned her to face what he wanted her to see.

They were in Mac's studio. A painting had been propped on an easel at one end of the room, the picture waiting to dry and be framed. Mac had set the lights so that the picture was illuminated, the rest of the room shadowed. Isabella saw that he'd already put into use the brush holder studded with semiprecious stones she'd given him this morning, but her attention was all for the new painting.

The picture showed Aimee in a pretty white dress, the skirt pulled back over a tiny bustle, her plump legs encased in white stockings and little black high-button shoes. She leaned casually on a chair and looked down at the fiery-haired Eileen, who was seated on it, her arms around her baby brother Robbie. Eileen grinned out of the picture, and Robbie gazed at the painter—his father —with curiosity and good humor.

Achilles, the heroic dog, lay with head up in front of the chair, on watch. Fergus, the little white terrier, had his feet on the chair, mouth lolling in a smile at the children.

"I hadn't meant to paint in the dogs," Mac said. "But when I was doing the preliminary drawings, the bloody animals wouldn't leave."

He'd depicted them in a garden, though Isabella

knew he'd likely done all the sittings right here. The picture was full of bright summer flowers and twining vines, the landscape flowing into recognizable mountains, the ones near Kilmorgan.

The colors were vivid, and a large pitcher on the ground held a bouquet of yellow roses. The yellow roses shouted *Mac painted this*, even over the casually scrawled *Mackenzie* in the bottom corner.

Isabella pressed her hands together, eyes blurring with tears. Her children, two she'd had with Mac, one adopted to save from a wretched life, were bright and beautiful on the canvas. Mac had captured them as only Mac could, not stiffly posed, but laughing and playing as they loved to.

"Oh, Mac, it's the most beautiful thing I've ever seen."

"A bit slapdash," Mac said in his careless way. "Our children do not like sitting still. The dogs were better behaved."

Isabella turned in his arms, even if it meant she had to look away from the wonderful painting.

"Don't you dare belittle that picture. It is beautiful, the best thing you've ever done."

"I don't know. There was a Venetian view that I thought turned out rather well—"

Isabella placed her fingers over Mac's mouth. "Stop."

He grinned, eyes shining. "I was teasing. The Venetian paintings were bloody awful."

"Shush," Isabella said, her voice softer.

She lifted her fingers away and replaced them with her lips. "I love you, Mac Mackenzie." She kissed him again. "Thank you. It's a marvelous gift." One straight from his heart.

Mac slid his arms around her. "The ball is beginning," he reminded her, but his voice was low, coaxing, his smile hot.

"Bother the ball," Isabella said, and drew her husband close once more.

CAMERON DANCED WELL, LOUISA OBSERVED FROM where she sat against the gilded wall next to her mother. He swung Ainsley around in exuberance, her gown billowing, his kilt pressing her legs. He danced closer than decorum decreed, even between husband and wife —especially between husband and wife these days. Husbands were meant to leave their baser needs to their mistresses.

Very silly, Louisa thought. She'd seen how happy Isabella had grown under Mac's rather indecorous attentions. Anytime Isabella was caught kissing her husband, she blushed rosy pink, but not with shame.

Come to think of it, Isabella and Mac weren't in the ballroom at all. Ian and Beth stayed in a corner, Beth conversing with Elliot McBride and his wife, Ian drinking whiskey and pretending to converse. Louisa craned to look around the room. Ainsley and Cameron danced, Hart strolled about, talking to guests alone, Eleanor having retreated again to her bedchamber. Daniel . . .

"Dance with me, Louisa."

Daniel didn't give Louisa much chance to refuse. He

pulled her to her feet and swung her into the waltz in the space of a breath.

He danced with the exuberance of his father, but with the vigor of a boy. Louisa spun around and around, and she began to laugh.

"Did you feel sorry for me?" Louisa asked. "The poor wallflower?" Wallflowers were able to observe much, however, such as which gentlemen might be eligible at the marriage mart come spring.

"No, I saw a beautiful woman who should dance. Ah, Louisa, if I were a wee bit older . . ."

"You would still not be ready for courting," Louisa finished.

Daniel laughed. "Aye, that's so. I have a few wild oats to sow yet."

Louisa laughed with him. It was impossible not to like Danny. "Not the most complimentary thing to tell a young woman who's condescended to dance with you."

"No, but you're family. I have no secrets from you."

"I'm not sure whether to be flattered or frightened."

"Flattered, love. It's not everyone gets to be welcomed into this family. Most run far from us or refuse to like us. Can't think why."

"You're ridiculous, Daniel Mackenzie."

"Ah, she cuts me to the quick. You are lovely, Louisa. Remember that. Worthy of any gentleman who chooses you. And the Mackenzie family embraces you with open arms."

Louisa's eyes narrowed. She wondered whether Isabella had spread the news that Louisa wanted to marry, but she squelched the thought. Isabella wasn't one to betray confidences from her sister.

No, she wasn't sure what Daniel had in mind. She also noticed he'd danced her to the far end of the ballroom, near the open doors to the corridor beyond. The music ceased, the dancers applauded the musicians, and they drifted from the floor to wait for the next set, probably a Scottish reel Louisa still hadn't learned.

"Shall I fetch you an ice?" Daniel asked. "Walk ye back to your mother? Kiss you in the corridor? The mistletoe is just there, see?" He pointed to the sprig hanging down from the chandelier in the middle of the deserted hall.

"No, thank you, to any of those," Louisa said. "I hear the fiddles going for a Scottish tune, which you might want to run off and join."

Daniel stood tall and looked down his nose at her. "A gentleman does not desert a lady."

"This lady prefers to walk in the cool hall a moment, alone. You do rather dance one's breath away, Danny."

Daniel executed a deep bow, ruining his dignified look by breaking into a wide grin. "M' heart shatters that you send me away, but never let it be said I pushed my attentions onto an unwilling lady. Good evening, dear Aunt-in-law."

So saying he whirled, kilt swinging, and ran back for the ballroom, narrowly missing a footman carrying a tray of champagne.

Louisa walked on down the hall, trying to slow her breathing. She'd sent Daniel away not only because she wanted to recover from the dance, but because she'd glimpsed a man in black disappear down this hall, one who looked like a Mackenzie and not at the same time.

But he'd vanished, to her disappointment. Ah, well.

Probably for the best. But it would have been nice to speak to him one last time before she and Mama departed for London to prepare for the Season.

Perhaps he'd gone into the sitting room at the end of the short hall, beckoning with its open doors. She avoided the place where the mistletoe hung and made for the sitting room, satin skirts in hand.

The room was empty. A fire had been lit here for the guests, but the guests remained in the colorful ballroom. The hall bent beyond the sitting room, she saw, ending in a flight of dark steps leading upward.

Louisa hid a sigh. Likely Mr. Fellows had gone upstairs, retiring to his chamber. She knew that he felt a bit out of place among the Mackenzie guests, as Louisa sometimes did herself.

She turned firmly away, ready to return to her mother and put the man out of her mind . . . and ran straight into Mr. Fellows.

"Oh." The word escaped Louisa's mouth before she could stop it. "I mean, good evening, Mr. Fellows."

Fellows took a step back, then he bowed, the bow stiff, as though he forced himself to remember conventional politeness. "Lady Louisa."

"It's . . . well . . . I . . . ." At supper she'd been able to be gracious and decorous, but now her polish and training deserted her. She roved her gaze over him, trying frantically to think of something to say, then she looked again. "You're wearing a kilt."

Mr. Fellows spoke in his usual dry tone. "Hart Mackenzie's gift to me."

"You weren't wearing it at supper."

"His wife persuaded me to don it for the ballroom.

However I doubt there will be any Scottish dancing for me."

"Nor for me. I haven't yet mastered the steps."

Mr. Fellows cleared his throat. "Then perhaps you would like to sit?"

He gestured to the chairs placed about inside the sitting room, each of them a polite distance from the others.

Mr. Fellows did not want to sit down with Louisa. She saw that in his stance, in the tightness around his eyes, in the way he wouldn't look directly into her face.

Louisa remained where she was in the doorway. "Such a shame that you must return to London tomorrow. That you cannot spend New Year's with us."

"Unfortunately, the criminals of London do not stop for the holidays. I have a continuing investigation for which my governor wants a result before the new year."

"Perhaps we shall see you in London in January, then. Mama and I will be spending the Season there. With Isabella and Mac."

"Perhaps," Fellows said, his voice going still more dry. Unlikely that a Scotland Yard inspector would cross paths with a society miss. He knew this, as did she.

"Yes, well." Louisa fell silent, and he went quiet as well.

How foolish, Louisa's rapid thoughts went. Two grownup people with connections to the same family, standing and staring at each other. Surely we can speak of the weather if nothing else.

But no sound came from her throat. Louisa knew that when Mr. Fellows walked away, when he left the house early in the morning to begin his journey south, she would not see him again. Not for a long time, and then only at family gatherings where they'd again be awkward and overly polite.

A burst of song came down the hall—fiddles and pipes, the beat of a drum. Guests laughed and clapped. Louisa should return, should sit with her mother, dance with other gentlemen, make herself agreeable.

She couldn't move. Louisa opened her mouth to make an inane remark to Mr. Fellows, anything to keep the conversation going, and found him looking up at the doorway in which they stood.

Someone had hung mistletoe in it. Louisa had made a wide berth around the sprig that hung in the hall, but in her quest to find Mr. Fellows, she'd not seen this one.

He looked at her for a frozen moment. Louisa's words died, every lesson that governesses and finishing school had pounded into her evaporating.

She only knew that a strong man stood with her, different from any gentleman she'd ever met. A cushion of music floated up the hall, canceling all other sound.

Louisa had kissed him before. She remembered the pressure of his mouth, the taste of his lips. She, the forward thing, had coerced him into kissing her.

Louisa grasped the lapels of his coat, rose on her tiptoes, and caught his mouth in another kiss. Mr. Fellows stiffened under her touch, ready to pull away.

Then something in him changed. His mouth formed to hers, responding, and his arms flowed around her.

He tasted of whiskey and the acrid bite of smoke. Hard arms enfolded her, crushing her against the flat planes of his body. No hesitant kisses of a gentleman wanting to court a lady—Fellows kissed her in hunger, in need.

Desperation fluttered in Louisa's heart. His mouth opened hers, pressing inside her, demanding, wanting.

She hung on to him, her fingers curling into his coat, tears wetting the corners of her eyes. He kissed like a madman, with hot desire, a forbidden taste of what she could never have.

He released her, his eyes glittering with anger, but not at her. "Louisa," he whispered.

Louisa tightened her grip on his coat, wanting to come against him again, needing to feel his strong body against hers. He slid a hand under her hair . . .

A crowd of laughing, flushed dancers poured from the ballroom and headed down the hall for the mistletoe in the middle. Daniel's voice rose over the others—" Don't all rush at once. It's only a little wager."

Fellows released Louisa and faded from her. One moment, she saw him in the shadows of the staircase, the next, he was gone.

Louisa put her hand to her hair and gulped deep breaths. The imprint of his mouth lingered on her lips, the bite of his fingers on her back. She could barely stand, her legs weak and hot.

But the others were coming. Louisa pasted on a smile and moved on shaking legs to meld with the crowd and pretend she'd been part of it all along.

"Don't disappoint me, Dad," Daniel said the next day.

Cameron shot his son a half-teasing, half-annoyed look and moved to the middle of the ballroom.

Garlands still hung the walls, draped the windows, and dripped from the chandeliers. Gone were the orchestra, dancers' finery, and footmen circulating with champagne; in their place were men in kilts, women in plaid gowns, the English guests in casual clothes that indicated they'd next take a tramp in the garden. The footmen, who had the day off, lounged with the maids on the other side of the room, and tea, coffee, and champagne had been set up on a long table for the guests to serve themselves.

Ainsley pressed her hands together and tried not to obviously ogle her husband. Cameron had stripped down to shirtsleeves, kilt, wool socks, and soft shoes. Bellamy wore the same except he had close-fitting breeches rather than a kilt.

Cameron, with his athletic, tall body, was a fine specimen, and Ainsley tried not to think too hard about what that body looked like under his clothing. Other ladies of the party cast glances at the men and whispered, Cameron drawing as many gazes as Bellamy.

At one time, Ainsley would have burned with jealousy. Cameron had made it known, however, that his rakehell days were over. No more mistresses, a different one every six-month, no more trysts with other men's wives. He was married, and happily so. Besides, Eleanor, in charge of the guest lists, had the good taste not to invite any ladies who'd once shared a bed with Cameron Mackenzie.

Cameron's Christmas gift to her revealed his more thoughtful side—a beautiful ebony and mother-of-pearl box in which to keep Ainsley's embroidery things. Cam had expressed puzzlement at first that Ainsley *made* things when she could afford to buy them, but he'd come to understand that the act of embroidering was special to her. He'd been equally pleased with the gift she'd given him—a horse blanket she'd sewn herself for his favorite horse, Jasmine. Their private exchange of gifts had been a most satisfying occasion.

David Fleming had agreed to referee the match before he returned to England in pursuit of Ian's Ming bowl. Daniel was busy coordinating the many wagers, which he'd gathered with ruthless efficiency. Hart, when he'd agreed that Bellamy and Cameron could have the match, had stipulated that it should be for amusement only, no wagering.

Hart must have known everyone would ignore him. Ainsley had placed a nice sum on her husband, but she knew the servants had bet heavily on Bellamy.

Perhaps too heavily. Some of them looked worried as they waited anxiously for the event to begin.

Bellamy, however, was in fine form. Though he'd not fought in years, he'd managed to keep his strength and steadiness. Against a skilled opponent Daniel's age, Bellamy might come to grief, but he and Cameron, both in their thirties, both honed from exercise, and both experienced, were well matched.

"Gentlemen," David said, standing between them. "You'll box until I call time in each round. Then you'll break apart until I call time again. If a man falls and stays down for a count of ten, he will be considered defeated. Shake hands, make it a fair fight."

Cameron and Bellamy shook, each confident, each wishing the other well. Then they broke apart.

"Very well, then," David said. "Gentlemen. Fight."

CHAPTER THIRTEEN

*T*he room exploded with noise.

The two men began by circling each other, looking for a weakness, a chance to get in the first hit.

Ainsley held her breath, suddenly nervous. It was one thing to imagine her husband in a splendid fight, another to wait for an equally large man to strike him.

Bellamy punched first. He did it with quick efficiency, but Cameron was ready and blocked the blow. Cameron sidestepped and came back into place, throwing a sudden jab at Bellamy's jaw. Bellamy blocked that and countered, which Cameron blocked in turn.

They stepped apart but swiftly came together again, each having the measure of the other. The punches began in earnest, Bellamy with a powerful, straight fist, Cameron moving under his guard and getting in a quick jab. Shouting escalated as the match moved from polite entertainment to serious combat.

Ainsley could see Bellamy's professionalism—his emotionless expression, his watchfulness, the way he avoided what looked like easy openings. Cameron didn't have as much experience in the ring, but he'd taken lessons from professional trainers, as many gentlemen did, and he'd fought at university and in impromptu matches in England, Scotland, France, and other parts of the Continent.

Steven McBride stood at Ainsley's elbow. Her youngest brother had seen much true fighting in the army, in bloody battles in India and the Middle East. All Ainsley's brothers save Patrick had spent time in the army, shaped by their years far from home. Elliot had left the army to run a business in India before his capture, Sinclair had sold his commission to marry and take up a profession, but Steven would likely be a career officer.

"Oh, good move," Steven said when Cameron landed a punch on Bellamy's jaw. "Nice feint."

"Come on then, Bellamy," Curry's voice rose over the noise. "I've got me Christmas wages on you. 'E's only a lordship. Ye can take 'im."

"After him, Dad!" Daniel yelled. "Did ye nae see that coming? Block. *Block*."

The cacophony rose, the family and guests yelling for Cameron, the servants for Bellamy. Not all the guests shouted for Cam, Ainsley noted. Some had bet on the sure thing of the professional pugilist.

Ainsley heard herself shouting right along with everyone else, bouncing on her toes as her husband landed punch after punch, driving Bellamy across the room. Cameron paid for it as soon as Bellamy recovered and retaliated. Cameron danced back on light feet, Bellamy following him, fists flying.

The duke's grand ballroom—the very room in which

Eleanor and Hart had married—became a back-street boxing ring, the guests abandoning their politeness, the Scots servants shouting insults at their masters with good-natured vigor.

"Now, then, your lordship, are you going to let your-self be beat by a Sassenach?" "Aye, he's good with a horse, but not with a fist." "We're counting on you, Bellamy, even if ye are a bloody Englishman."

Cameron wore a slight smile as he fought. He loved this, Ainsley saw. He was a physical man, leaving the thinking problems like mathematics and business to Ian and Hart. He loved horses, women, fighting, gambling. And now Ainsley and his daughter—with all his might. Cameron didn't hold back on anything.

"What's he doing?" Steven said in her ear.

Ainsley studied Cameron, who was busily avoiding Bellamy's blows. "What do you mean?"

"He's . . . it's as if he's trying to lose."

Ainsley didn't understand what Steven saw, but Steven must know what he was talking about. To Ains-ley, Cameron was blocking and punching, wheeling and dancing, just as Bellamy was.

David called time for the first round, and the two broke apart. Daniel sped in to give his father a sip of water, a cloth for his face. The rest period didn't last long, and the fight resumed.

Again, Ainsley saw nothing but two men doing their best to pummel each other, but Steven told her differ-ently. "Ah, a fine hit. Looks like Cam was waiting for that opening. Good man. But he could have ended it just then, and he didn't."

"Perhaps he wants us to have a good show," Ainsley said.

"Maybe he's worried about the servants losing their pay packets."

True. Both servants and guests had started betting thick and fast as soon as the fight was announced.

It would be just like Cameron to let Bellamy win the fight and spare the servants losing their wages. Hart's guests could stand the loss, but the servants, some of whom contributed their packets to large families, could not. Cameron would think it fitting to provide entertainment and make sure Hart's staff took money from the duke's guests.

Cam was a generous man beneath his hard exterior, something Ainsley had understood soon after she'd come to know him. He never boasted, and was often under-handed or reckless in his generosity, but his big heart encompassed all.

I love you, Cameron Mackenzie. He'd showed a side of himself to Ainsley that no one else knew about. Their secret.

Bellamy beat Cameron across the floor again, the servants screaming for their favorite. Ainsley cupped her hands around her mouth and shouted, "Cam! I love you!"

Cameron's grin widened, but the acknowledgment cost him a blow. Bellamy landed one on his face, and Cameron tripped. The crowd on his side of the room groaned.

Cameron regained his feet without falling and coun-tered with a punch to Bellamy's jaw. Bellamy's head snapped back, and now the servants groaned.

Cameron waited, fists ready, for Bellamy to come at him again, but Bellamy staggered. Ainsley watched him in surprise. The punch hadn't been hard, Cameron still trying to find his balance. Ainsley had seen that even without Steven's confirmation.

Bellamy took a step back, faltered, took another step to catch himself, and then he fell backward, his eyes rolling up into his head. As the shouting rose, Bellamy landed on the parquet floor with a loud *whump*.

David, startled, came forward and began to count him out.

"Aw, Bellamy," Curry shouted. "You bastard. Get up, will ye?"

Bellamy stirred, but David reached ten while Bellamy lay on the floor, not attempting to rise.

"Cameron Mackenzie, winner," David said, a bewildered note in his voice.

The Mackenzie guests shouted their victory. The servants groaned and booed. Cameron stood with hands on his hips, staring down at Bellamy while Mac knelt beside his valet to minister to him.

A woman darted out of the crowd—Esme, who'd been given a job here at Bellamy's insistence—and fell to her knees at Bellamy's side. Bellamy's eyes swam open as Esme bent over him and lifted his bruised head into her lap. Bellamy smiled up at her, looking happy.

Ainsley went to Cameron, and he put an unsteady arm around her shoulders. "Damn him," he said. "He went down so a lady would be all over him w' sympathy, the crafty beggar. That was *my* plan."

"I know." Ainsley wrapped her arm around him,

feeling his body shudder with reaction to the fight, its abrupt end, his hurts. "You're a wonderful man."

Cameron ruffled her hair with a shaking hand. "What do you mean, you know? How? Did it show?"

"Steven told me you were pulling your punches, trying to let Bellamy win. I knew it was the sort of thing you'd do."

"Damn and blast." Cameron wiped sweat from his eyes. "He would have beaten me fair, even if I hadn't held back. He's a hell of a fighter."

The servants on the other side of the room surrounded Bellamy, their fallen champion. A few shot Cameron evil looks.

"They do not look happy," Cam said. "They'll put sand in my soup, I shouldn't wonder."

"Can you blame them? They've lost money they couldn't afford to."

"No, they haven't." Cameron released Ainsley and called to his son, who was crowing that his father had beaten a London champion.

"Good fighting, Dad," Daniel said when he'd loped over.

"If you say so. I want you to cancel all the bets. Give everyone their money back."

"What?" Daniel blinked, mouth open. "I can't do that. I'll be mobbed."

"You'll lose your percentage, you mean," Cameron growled at him. "No one loses today," he said in a loud voice to the rest of the room. Talking ceased, heads turned to see what the winner was saying. "Daniel is returning your money. Bet on my horses. It's safer."

As surprised then angry murmurs rose from the guests, Cameron lifted his hand.

"The money is returned, or I can go to the duke and tell him his orders about betting were ignored. Ye can argue with Hart, or ye can take your money and be done."

The murmurs ceased, and guests drifted off, annoyed, but the servants cheered. "Thank ye, sir," one shouted, and "'E's a proper gent, I always said," came from Curry.

Daniel sighed and drew a pouch out of his sporran. "You'll ruin me, Dad."

"I didn't raise you to be a bookmaker, Danny."

"But I'm good at it."

"That's what worries me."

Muttering under his breath, Daniel left them to circulate the crowd, his movements betraying his irritation.

Steven appeared and shook Cameron's hand. "Excellent fight. You know a thing or two."

"Aye, maybe I used to. Bellamy's tough. I'll stick to horses."

Steven grinned, pressed a kiss to Ainsley's cheek, and moved off. Cameron pulled Ainsley against him again. "Do you think they'll notice if the reigning champion slinks off to his soft bed to recover?"

"I think you might be forgiven."

Cameron's gaze heated. "Bellamy took a fall to win a woman. What shall I have to do?"

"You've already won her," Ainsley said. She laid her hand on his chest. "However, perhaps I should don my New Year's frock and see how you like it. The bodice has ever so many buttons."

"Wicked." Cameron brushed a kiss to her lips. "Mmph. Even kissing is painful. I believe I'll need my wife's healing touch."

"Yes, indeed," Ainsley said, and she led her husband away, up to their bedchamber, where all was quiet, and bliss.

DAVID FLEMING DEPARTED SOON AFTER THE FIGHT and didn't return until the thirtieth of December. By that time, all guests but family had gone, making the house party smaller but no less loud. Preparations went on for the Hogmanay celebration, which would include another feast, bonfires, and a walk to the village to join in the celebrations there. Beth, Ainsley, and Isabella visited the less fortunate with baskets heaped with food, blankets, and clothing. Eleanor fretted that she couldn't be part of the good works, but she could at least help fill the baskets as she waited for her child to be born.

David was well into inebriation as he rolled out of the carriage that had been sent to fetch him from the train. Hart met him in the foyer, and David thrust a box into Hart's waiting hands as soon as he walked in the front door.

David's face was drawn, his eyes heavy with fatigue. Hart steered him into his downstairs study and closed the door.

"You look like hell," Hart said.

"You would too after the few days I've had. That is to say, nights." David glanced at the whiskey decanter, always kept full, and shuddered.

"I've sent for coffee." Hart touched the box on his desk. "This is it?"

"The very one." David sank into a chair. "Dearly bought."

Hart let his voice warm. "Well done."

David blinked. "Praise from Hart Mackenzie? I must make a note in my diary."

"Kiss my fundament," Hart said dryly. "How did you manage it?" He leaned against his desk and crossed his ankles. "I admit, I'm curious."

David started to laugh. Before he could answer, a footman entered with a silver coffee pot and porcelain cups on a tray, which he placed on a table at David's elbow, and then departed. David's laughter tapered off as he poured himself a cup of steaming black liquid.

"The earl loves the ladies," David said, lifting the cup.

"We all do."

"Ah, but he loves them in a special way." David blew steam from the surface of the coffee and took a sip. "Was a while before I twigged. All suggestions, subtle or blatant, that we avail lovely women of our skills in bed was met with cold disapproval. Until I realized that what Prudy Preston likes is not to touch, but to watch."

Hart listened in surprise. "He's a voyeur?" He'd met more than one gentleman in his lifetime who gained pleasure by watching others find it, but he'd never suspected it of the prim and proper Earl of Glastonby.

David chuckled and took another sip of coffee. "The tale grows more intriguing. He's not interested in watching a bloke and his ladylove having a go. He enjoys watching ladies with each other." He closed his eyes. "Oh, it was delicious to discover that."

Hart didn't ask how David had convinced Glastonby to tell him—David was famous for winnowing out of people things they didn't want others to know.

"Once I discovered his guilty secret, it was easy to orchestrate an encounter for him," David went on. "I knew two young ladies who were all too eager to help. Yesterday afternoon, I escorted Glastonby to a house where the ladies put on quite a show for him. I rather enjoyed it. He wouldn't touch them—oh, no—he thinks himself too good for the likes of women such as they. But he let them perform. Lapped it up, shall we say." Another sip, David beginning to relax.

Glastonby was exactly the sort of man Hart loathed—one who detested the same women he used to gain his pleasure. When Hart had lived in his own personal bawdy house, he'd taken plenty of pleasure in the young women who lived there with him, though Hart recognized now that he'd never let down his guard, never not been in charge of every move in the bed.

But he'd never despised the women in his house for being paid courtesans, or submissive to him. Hart had recognized that they were people in their own right, with hopes and troubles, despair and delights. The young women had often asked his advice about whatever concerned them—or about life itself—and when they wanted to leave, Hart would send them off with enough money to ensure their survival.

"What did you do to him?" Hart asked. "Something nasty, I hope."

"Of course, old friend." David sent him a smile that did not bode well for the Earl of Glastonby. "What should happen as we were taking our rest, the young ladies still intertwined in the drawing room, but that a vicar should happen to call, with every intent of reforming said young women? This vicar beheld, to his shock, the upright Earl of Glastonby with his trousers undone, the earl, whose wife leads so many reform committees. Stifling my laughter was painful, I assure you."

"This vicar was your old friend?"

"All too glad to expose a sinner. Dr. Pierson has a fine sense of humor, I am happy to say. A truly good man—there aren't many. By the way, you owe him five hundred guineas for his church roof fund. They'll be able to start their repairs thanks to your generous—and anonymous—donation."

"I'll have Wilfred draw him a cheque when he returns," Hart said without changing expression.

"I told Glastonby I could square it with the vicar to keep silent, especially to his wife and the earl's upright friends. My price, one Ming bowl. Glastonby took me to his house and nearly threw the bowl at me. I'll never be received in his home again." David laughed in delight. "Thank God."

Hart relaxed. The ever-reliable David had done his job. "You're a devious snake," Hart said.

"Indeed," David gave him a modest nod. "I was taught by the master—Lord Hart Mackenzie, now the lofty Duke of Kilmorgan. You might know him." He drained the last of the coffee from the cup and rose. "Shall we deliver the gift to Beth? Let me hand it to her. *I* want her kiss of gratitude."

~

IAN REMOVED THE FIRST LAYER OF PAPER THEN OF straw, feeling Beth's breath on his cheek. The warmth of it made him want to push the box aside and lead her away from all the people who'd gathered in the dining room. Why did they hover as though whatever Hogmanay gift Beth wanted to give him was any of their business?

He carefully lifted out another layer of straw and set it aside. His brothers, their wives, Daniel, David, Louisa, the McBrides, and Beth, leaned forward.

Inside the wooden box, nestled on another layer of straw, lay a Ming bowl. Ian lifted it out with gentle fingers—one never knew with porcelain how brittle it had become over the years.

It was a decent specimen, a bit small, but with finely painted dragons flowing among vine leaves. A chrysanthemum decorated the bottom of the outside. The blue was good, not as brilliant as the Russian gentleman's bowl, but a similar shade.

"This was the Earl of Glastonby's," Ian said, turning the bowl in his hands. He sniffed the porcelain—it was authentic. Some aristocrats in need of money had copies of their antiques made before they sold the originals, then forgot to mention that what they owned was the copy. Ian had seen this bowl before, when Glastonby had opened his home to show his collection, to raise money for one of his wife's charitable works. "He refused to sell it to me."

"I know," David Fleming said. "Prying it out of him was an onerous chore, but one I happily performed."

"It wasn't necessary," Ian said. "It's not as good as many of my others."

Beth leaned to him, distracting him again with the touch of her breath, her voice like an alto flute, the softness of her breasts against his shoulder. "Do you not like it?"

She wore the expression Ian had come to understand meant she was worried and trying not to show it. Worried about what? That he didn't want the bowl? Of course, he wanted it. Ming bowls were his passion.

"I will add it to my collection."

Ian thought his answer would close the matter, but his family remained staring at him, and Beth's expression grew more anxious. "It is like the one I broke." She touched the design. "With the dragons, and the flowers, and the blue."

What was she talking about? This bowl was nothing like that one—perhaps it was similar in design and color, but with a completely different character and age.

"It isn't the same," Ian said, trying to make Beth understand. "The leaves on the vines are different, and at the bottom is a mum, not a dragon. This bowl is about fifty years newer than the other." He carefully returned it to the straw. He'd have to rearrange the collection a little to fit it in, but no matter.

Hart broke in. "I'm sorry, Ian. My fault. I thought it would suffice."

Suffice for what? A new bowl was always welcome, and the fact that Beth had tried to buy him one warmed him.

"Are you saying this is *not* the one you wanted?" David asked, his voice too loud for Ian's taste. "Not that I didn't enjoy my task, but are you not the least bit happy we wrested a prized possession from Glastonby? Now you have it, and he doesn't."

Words began to knock together in Ian's head. He couldn't follow the undercurrents of the conversation, and his old frustration started to rise.

"If I'd wanted Glastonby's bowl, I would have had it," Ian said.

David slid a flask from his pocket and took a drink. "But you just said he wouldn't sell it to you."

"He would have. Eventually. If I'd wanted him to."

Ian turned to Beth, ready for his family to go and leave them alone. He stopped, his confusion escalating, when he saw the tears in her blue eyes.

His brothers had drilled into him that, when someone gave him a present, Ian should acknowledge it. Perhaps that's what she was waiting for.

"Thank you, my Beth."

Beth swallowed, more tears moistening her eyes. "You're welcome, Ian."

Ian closed the box. End of the matter.

"Ian." Mac laid a heavy hand on Ian's shoulder. "A word with you, if you don't mind. Alone."

CHAPTER FOURTEEN

*I*an tried to ignore him. He didn't want to leave Beth, who was still crying. He wanted to kiss away her tears, to feel the moisture on her lashes brushing his lips. He needed to discover what was the matter, to make her happy again. He'd thought he'd done so with Jamie's Christmas gift, but he'd been wrong.

Mac's hand firmed. "Now."

Ian smothered a sigh, pushed the box away, rose from the table, and let Mac lead him out into the hall. The others closed on Beth—if they didn't leave her alone, they'd suffocate her.

"Ian." Mac shut the door, cutting off Ian's view of Beth. "Sometimes, my little brother, you can be incomparably cruel."

"What are you talking about?" This was what happened when his family wouldn't let Ian and Beth be alone. When Ian could wrap himself in Beth's presence, he was at peace, in a blissful place where all was stillness. Now there was turmoil, tears. "I said 'thank you'."

"How can I explain this? Beth feels terrible that she broke your blasted bowl. She's been hunting everywhere for one like it, Hart bullied half the country until he located a Ming bowl with blue dragons on it, and he sent Fleming to lure Glastonby into a compromising position so Glastonby would hand it over. Fleming rushed it to Hart, who rushed it to Beth, who rushed it to you. She wanted to make up for what she'd done. Do you see?"

"But the bowl was irreplaceable," Ian said. Perhaps if he spoke slowly, he could make himself clear. "It was very rare. Glastonby's is not as good."

"Not the point. Beth was very unhappy that she broke the bowl. She knew how much it meant to you. Hell, for months you wouldn't talk about anything else. And then she broke it. The woman who loves you broke it. How do you think that made her feel?"

"I know Beth was upset. I told her it was all right."

Mac scraped his hands through his hair. "Yes, yes, you *told* her. But every time she thought of a way to make up for it, you said she never could. You told Curry he needn't have bothered sticking the damn thing back together, as Beth asked him to. And now, she goes to the trouble of finding you another bowl, and you tell her it isn't good enough."

"It isn't as good. But I said I'd keep it . . ."

"And I want to break the bloody thing over your head. Focus, Ian. Look at me."

Ian shifted his gaze, which still rested on the door that blocked him from Beth, to Mac's copper-colored eyes.

"Beth is hurting," Mac said. "Because she thinks she hurt *you*."

Bewildering. "She didn't."

"But she doesn't know that."

Ian couldn't look away from Mac as his thoughts spun around and the events straightened out in his head. A mathematical problem. $A = x$ and $B = y$; if $A + B = C$, then $C = x + y$.

"She thinks she hurt me because she broke the bowl," Ian said.

"Yes!" Mac threw up his hands. "Ian wins the race."

"What race?"

"Never mind. Forget about races. Let's return to Beth being upset. You love your bowls, and Beth destroyed something you love." $A + B = C$. Except that A was flawed.

"I don't love the bowls."

"You're overly fond of them then."

"No." Ian thought a moment. "They please me." Uniform, their gentle shape, the intricacy of the designs.

"Fine. Beth destroyed something that pleased you. Therefore, she is unhappy."

Ian did not like Beth being unhappy. Her sorrow was his; he ached when he saw her tears.

Ian looked again at Mac, his unruly, teasing brother, the one he understood least. Mac was the opposite of Ian —he was impetuous, reckless, volatile, wild, whereas Ian needed his life to be neat and exact, his routine unbroken unless absolutely necessary. Mac's artistic talent had earned their father's wrath, and he'd run away from the cloying household at a young age. Ian's exactness had also earned his father's wrath, the old duke believing Ian mad, and punishing him for it.

"What do I do?" Ian asked. He was swimming, uncertain, trying to find the current.

"Tell Beth you're not upset at her for breaking the bowl. Simple as that."

"But I told her."

"Tell her again. And again. As many times as it takes for her to believe you. *Explain* why you are not upset. In great detail—you are good at details."

The dining room door was beckoning to him, because behind it lay Beth. All the bowls in the world could crumble to dust, and it wouldn't matter, because he could lean down and kiss Beth's cheek, smoother than any porcelain.

Talking to Beth was an excellent idea. Talking to her alone, an even better one.

He turned away from Mac, who let out another long sigh, and opened the door.

Beth looked up from the circle of family who were trying to comfort her. Ian went to her, ignoring all in his way, swept up the wooden box with the bowl in it, took Beth's hand, and tugged her back toward the door. Hart started to follow.

"No," Ian said. "Only Beth."

Hart, the man who'd helped Ian through his worst moments, gave him a hard look. Mac stepped in front of Hart, blocking his way. "Let him go."

Ian never broke stride. He took Beth down the hall, around the corner to their private wing, and up the stairs to the Ming room. Ruby, who'd been napping on the sunny landing, climbed noisily to her feet and followed them inside. All the dogs knew they were allowed only a foot or so inside the Ming room, so Ruby lay down again, blocking Ian's ability to close the door.

No matter. The entire wing was theirs, and he and Beth were alone.

Ian moved to a cabinet in the middle of the room, in which another bowl reposed, and set the box on top of it. "We'll put the new bowl here. *This* one will move to that space, and *that* one there." He pointed.

"How do you decide where to put them?" Beth asked. She still had tears on her face, but she spoke unwaveringly.

"Size, color, year." Ian touched the box. "This one belongs here."

"Ian." Beth stood close enough to him that he could breathe in her fragrance, but she didn't touch him. "If you don't want the bowl, I will have Hart return it to the earl."

Ian didn't answer. He let his gaze travel over the bowls in their cases, each perfect, exquisite, their presence like a ripple of cool water.

"Remember when I told you why I started collecting the bowls?"

Beth nodded. "You saw the first one in Paris, and it enchanted you."

"The world was a confusing place. Is a confusing place. I look at the bowls, and the confusion goes away. It gives me . . . silence."

"That's why I feel so awful, Ian. I took that away from you."

Ian traced a pattern on the box. "Focusing on the bowls helped blot out the darkness. I could sit here, I could look at them, and the darkness went away. For a little while." He looked up at Beth. "And then I met you."

She gave him a watery smile. "Do not tell me the darkness went away the moment you saw me. Flattering, but I know that is not true."

"It flowed away like an avalanche." Ian focused on her eyes, the blue he'd seen the night he'd met her. He'd known instantly that he needed this woman in his life, that she'd come to him like a gift from God. "And it's never returned. Not like before."

Beth's voice went soft. "I hope I have helped you. I love you. I *want* to help you."

She still wasn't understanding. "I don't need the bowls to give me peace anymore," Ian said. "I have you. And Jamie, and Belle. If all the Ming bowls in the world were smashed, I'd still have you." He took her hand, the one with the gold ring and band of sapphires he'd bought to replace the simple gold ring he'd slipped onto her finger when he'd married her in the Parisian pension. She still wore the simple gold with the more expensive one, and Ian kissed them both. "You broke the bowl, and it is gone. But *you* are here, and whole. Nothing else matters."

"Oh."

Ian once more let himself get lost in the blue of her eyes, the shape of her red lips, the way the moisture behind her lower lip made him want to lick her there. He'd kissed her many times since that first night at the opera, and he never grew tired of it.

He leaned down to kiss her now, but Beth put her fingers over his lips.

"Are you telling me that you don't care that I broke your bowl?" she asked.

Ian had thought they were finished with the discussion. "Yes," he said.

"But . . . it took so long for you to find it and cost so very much money."

Ian slid his hands to the curve of her waist. "I wanted to have it, because it reminded me of you," he said. "But I'd rather have you."

The uncertainty in Beth's eyes cleared, though they again swam with tears. She twined her arms around his neck. "Ian, I love you so much."

This was better. Much better. The darkness that had started to grip Ian, the one that told him he'd never learn how to make her happy, flowed away to nothing.

"My Beth." Ian looked straight into her eyes, letting himself be lost, not fighting it.

Beth kissed him, her lips shaking but warm, tasting of honey and her spice.

Ian opened her mouth with his, ready to taste her further, but she said, "I need to tell you something. I've meant to, but it never seemed the right time."

Ian waited, not asking. Beth would tell him, or she would not. Sometimes, she took a while to say what she needed to.

She wet her lips, making them all the more kissable. "Very soon, you'll have something else to remember me by. And to love." She leaned close, her voice dropping to a sweet whisper. "I'm going to have another baby."

That, Ian understood. He went still, and the world stopped with him. Then a wave of joy poured over him, sweeping away everything except Beth, her smile, and the words that she'd just spoken.

Ian picked her up off her feet and spun around with her. He felt his mouth stretching into a smile he couldn't stop, as he whirled his laughing wife around and around.

Ian at last set her down, Beth's face pink, her smile beautiful. The worried pucker between her brows was gone, Beth again in love with Ian.

Ian thought about the gestures Daniel made when he was excited. One seemed appropriate now.

Ian threw his arms straight up, his fists balling, and roared: *"Yes!"*

Ruby scrambled to her feet, barking, and the half-open door banged into the wall. Hart was there, filling the space. "Damn it, Ian. What happened?"

Hart, the interfering pain in the backside, had brought the whole family. Even Eleanor was there, behind Hart, leaning heavily on Daniel's arm.

No matter. Ian wanted to shout it to the world. "I'm going to be a father!"

"Again," Beth added quietly.

The tense silence burst into noise and laughter. The family poured in, Ruby swarming among them with her large body, her tail waving.

The ladies rushed to hug Beth; the Mackenzie brothers, Daniel, the McBrides, and David Fleming to clap Ian on the shoulders and shake him hard. Why good news involved the man being pounded, Ian had never understood, but he knew that the gestures made Mac, Cam, and Hart happy. Ian stood quietly and took their hand clasps, arms around his shoulders, liking that he was part of them, brothers who had never deserted him.

The shouting wound down to excited talking and laughter, still as noisy as only Ian's family could be. Beth had disappeared into a cloud of ladies' skirts, bustles, and laughter, and he heard Daniel say, "The wagering will open as soon as I fetch my books. No side betting, please, gentlemen," and Cameron's warning, *"Danny."*

"I'll put you down for a hundred then, shall I, Dad? Boy or girl?"

"Ian." Eleanor had broken from the feminine circle to pull Ian aside for a kiss. She had to use his arm to steady herself, but she was smiling and pink. "Beth told me why you weren't upset about the broken bowl. You really are the most romantic man in the world, do you know that? You ought to give your brothers lessons."

"I can hear you, El," Hart said from her other side.

"Yes, I know. Does that mean, Ian, that I could break another bowl, and it wouldn't matter?"

She reached toward a glass case, and Ian caught her wrist in sudden panic. "No!"

Eleanor laughed. "I am teasing you."

Ian's heart thumped as he released her. He didn't mind so much *Beth* breaking the stupid bowl, but no one else could. He gave up trying to make sense of them all, returning his thoughts to Beth and the brother or sister he would get to show Jamie and Belle.

"You know I'd never touch your exquisite bowls, Ian," Eleanor said. "They are yours, and I can be a bit clumsy, and . . . Ah." Eleanor's gaze became fixed, her face draining of color.

Hart stepped forward and steadied her. "I knew this was a bad idea," he growled. "Back to bed with you."

"Yes, I think that would be best." Eleanor swayed,

her hand going to the small of her back. "Perhaps we ought to hurry. I believe his little lordship is coming. *Right now.*"

As the words left her lips, Eleanor sagged, and she collapsed so swiftly that Hart barely had time to catch her and lift her into his arms.

CHAPTER FIFTEEN

*D*ark night came on—these days, the sun hardly appeared at all. To Hart the darkness and the cold matched his fear, as he paced the sitting room down the hall from Eleanor's bedchamber.

Ian was with him. Hart's quiet brother stood looking out the window at the blackness as Hart walked the room behind him. Restlessness bothered Ian and made him want to emulate it, so he'd learned to turn away and block it out.

Eleanor had decorated this room, making it a place in which they could be private after supper, or sit with family and close friends. Other members of the family had made their contributions: Ainsley had embroidered cushions with her neat skill to strew about the sofa; drawings done by Mac's children—Aimee's quite skilled, the others barely discernible scrawls—decorated the walls. Beth and Ian had purchased the long, comfortable sofa to replace the old-fashioned, overly carved horsehair one from the old duke's day.

A homey room, a room for family. Hart had never known such a retreat before his marriage.

"Damn it." He halted his pacing, sank to the sofa, and buried his head in his hands.

Eleanor's presence filled every corner of this room. If she did not live through the night . . .

There, he'd thought it. If she did not live, Hart would never enter this room again.

He smelled the sharp bite of whiskey and lifted his head to find Ian holding a glass out to him, brimful of Mackenzie malt.

Hart took the glass and poured half the contents down his throat. He coughed, wet his lips, and gulped down the other half.

Ian took the glass away and returned with it full again. Hart drank half of that before he sighed and set the whiskey on a table. His head spun, his gut churned, and still he feared.

A clock ticked on the mantelpiece, another pretty gift, this one from David Fleming. The clock chimed eleven, the fire burned, and Hart waited.

No news came. Hart and Ian didn't speak. The clock kept up its relentless ticking—chiming twelve, one. Finally Hart rose, stalked to the mantelpiece, ripped open the clock, and slapped its small pendulum to a halt. Only Ian's presence kept him from dashing the clock to the floor entirely.

"What is taking so confounded long?" Hart growled, staring at the now-still clock.

"Beth took a long time with Jamie," Ian said. "A day and a half. You can sleep if you want. I'll call you."

"Did you sleep?"

"No."

"Well, then." Hart resumed his pacing.

He did concede to eat something when Marcel carried in a light supper. Marcel also brought the news that Eleanor was in labor but the midwife did not believe she'd give birth for a while yet. Hart returned to moody contemplation, barely remembering to thank Marcel for his trouble. Marcel departed after Hart had downed a few mouthfuls, and Hart's gloom descended once more.

Now that he'd put the clock out of commission, Hart had to check his watch for time, which he found himself doing every five minutes. Another hour crawled by, and another.

Hart told Ian to go, but Ian stubbornly remained. Even when Beth entered, smudges of exhaustion on her face, and embraced Ian, Ian did not offer to leave.

Hart couldn't make his lips move to form questions to Beth, or his legs unbend to rise from the sofa. Beth came to Hart, sat next to him, and took his hand. Always a bad sign, when a woman did that.

"Eleanor is very strong," Beth said.

"What does that mean?" Hart snapped. He heard the rage and impatience in his voice, but he couldn't take the time to apologize.

"The baby is ready to come, but Eleanor's body is being slow to make the passage wide enough. It happens. The midwife is certain she'll come through it, and the baby will be born without trouble. It's just taking time."

"Tell me what it really means. If she can't birth naturally . . ."

"Then we send for a surgeon. But it's early days, yet."

Hart's body went numb. He couldn't feel, couldn't move. "If they have to cut the baby out, El could die."

"Surgery has progressed in the last years, and you have the best surgeon in the Highlands waiting to be sent for if needed. She'll be in good hands."

But surgery was always risky, because though the surgeon might do a fine job, the wound could become infected, or Eleanor could lose so much blood that she wouldn't be strong enough to live.

Eleanor would die.

The thought whirled around in Hart's head and through his stomach, sloshing with whiskey and what little he'd managed to eat, and made him sick.

Hart stood up abruptly, throwing off Beth's helpful clasp, and ran out of the room. His old bedchamber smelled stuffy and cloying, but the bathroom that opened from it had a working cistern. Here Hart lost all the whiskey and dinner Marcel had brought to the bowels of the house.

He rinsed his mouth, dabbing his lips with a towel. When he left the bathroom, he found Ian waiting for him in the bedroom.

"Where's Beth?" Hart asked him.

"Back to Eleanor."

"You don't have to stay with me." Hart looked around his old bedchamber with its monstrously high ceiling, paintings of gods and horses around the frieze, and its old and chunky furniture. This had been his father's bedchamber—the dukes of Kilmorgan had slept here since the house had been built.

"Ian, if I lose her." Hart wandered to the bed he'd abandoned months ago to move into Eleanor's cozier bedchamber down the hall. "Losing Sarah and my boy was the hardest thing I've ever lived through. But even then, you see, I knew that Eleanor was with me. If not *here*, then at least in the world, where I could find her. I could think of her living in that old house with her father, I could write to her if I chose. She was the anchor in my world, no matter how far I was from her. But if I lose *her* . . . Ian, I lose myself. I can't live. Not without Eleanor."

Ian listened with his usual expression—focused, brows slightly drawn, mouth straight—saying nothing. Whether he followed Hart's words or not, Hart didn't know. He never knew, with Ian.

He looked up at the ceiling. "God, I hate this room. I'm removing all furniture to the scrap heap and tearing out those bloody awful paintings. After . . ."

Ian held out his large hand to Hart. "Come with me."

"Come with you where?" Hart wasn't in the mood for expeditions.

Ian said nothing. He never explained. He simply expected Hart to trust him.

Hart gave up and followed his brother out of the room. Ian didn't go far. He led Hart down the hall to the chamber in which Eleanor lay and pushed open the door without knocking.

Hart smelled closeness, heat, the bite of the coal fire, too many people in a room with no fresh air, and blood. The room was too dark, too stuffy.

A maid swung around, alarm in her eyes. "You can't be in here, Your Grace. Your lordship."

The room teemed with women, maids in caps and aprons, the plump midwife, the wet nurse with her own baby, waiting to take Eleanor's. Beth sat on a chair on one side of the bed, holding Eleanor's hand.

Eleanor lay on her back, the covers bunched around her to form a kind of nest. Her arms, shoulders, and breasts were covered with her dressing gown, the rest of her exposed. Her knees were up, her skin dripping with sweat, her eyes closed in a pale face.

"Not really the place for you, Your Grace," the midwife said, without turning from the foot of the bed. "We'll let you men folk know when the time is right."

Eleanor opened her eyes. Hart thought she might call to him, but her face distorted, and she emitted a long wail that ended in a scream. Her body arched, spasms wracking it.

She fell back to the bed, breathless. Beth stroked her hand, her attention all for Eleanor. Eleanor gasped for a few seconds, then she wailed again.

Hart was across the room, pushing aside the maids, reaching for Eleanor. Eleanor moaned again, her head moving on the pillow, but she grasped Hart's outstretched hand and held it hard. More than hard. She squeezed it to the bone.

She fell back again, spent. "Hart."

"I'm here, El."

"Really, Your Grace. It's not fitting." The midwife, a large Scotswoman with fire-red hair, put her hands on her hips. Hart might be a duke, but this was her demesne.

"Please, let him stay," Eleanor said. "Please."

Hart read the pain in her blue eyes, the fear, the hope. He kissed her fingers, her hands so pitifully swollen.

"Beth says it shouldn't be long now," Eleanor whispered.

Hart saw, out of the corner of his eye, the midwife and Beth exchange a glance. They'd lied to soothe her.

"Good," Hart said. "That's good."

Ian, saying nothing, came around the bed, dragged a chair next to Beth's, and sat down. He took Beth's hand in his, leaned back, and closed his eyes.

Hart knew Eleanor's fears and shared them. She was thirty-three, this was her first child, and first children could be difficult. Eleanor was much more robust than Hart's first wife had been, but childbirth was dangerous in any case.

Hart had taken far too long to find Eleanor again. They'd had less than a year together, and he might lose her tonight.

Eleanor squeezed his hand, this time gently. "Are you all right, my love? You look a bit green."

"Which is why husbands should wait outside," the midwife said. "They're not good with what a woman can take in her stride."

"I'm fine," Hart snarled. "I . . ." He swallowed, forcing the bile down. "I'm fine, love."

"Good," Eleanor said. "I'm fine too." She closed her eyes, drawing a deep breath, and then her body went slack.

"What's the matter with her?" Hart asked in alarm.

The midwife looked harassed, but Beth answered. "She's only asleep. She's been drifting off from time to time. It's all right. Sleep is good for her. Gives her some peace."

But Eleanor looked too wan, her face too waxen for Hart's comfort.

The night wore on. There was another confounded clock in here, ticking, ticking. Eleanor woke up, groaning in pain, but the midwife still shook her head. Not yet.

Eleanor drifted off again, moaning a little in her sleep. Ian stayed with Beth, holding her hand as he dozed.

Hart stroked Eleanor's hand, wishing he could take all the pain away. In the days before his marriage to Eleanor, he'd spent time with women who liked Hart to inflict pain on them—to bind them and command them, and to use the pain, binding, and words to drive them to pleasure. He'd been good at it. Hart had mastered the technique of squeezing a woman's throat just enough so that when air cut off, her climax was that much more robust. A dangerous practice, but Hart had had the touch.

But he'd always been the master. He could twist and take, but when it was time to stop and soothe away the hurt, Hart had done it. He'd been excellent at that as well.

He looked at the woman he loved most in the world, knowing he couldn't take away her hurt, couldn't help her, and it killed him. Hart Mackenzie, the specialist in ultimate control and exquisite pleasures, could do nothing to relieve his wife.

Not true, he realized—he could do a few things. When Eleanor swam again to wakefulness, he got up onto the bed beside her, where he could snake his hands behind her back and gently rub it. He massaged there then worked his way up to knead her neck, and then her scalp.

Hart knew how to soothe, how to bring a woman down from unbearable ecstasy. He used the same movements as he glided his hands to her wrists, then to her ankles and back up her calves, trying to take away pain.

Eleanor, who knew what he was doing, smiled at him, her eyes heavy lidded. "I love being married to a wicked husband."

Hart gently kissed her lips. He'd spent many years mastering the art of cruelty, but then he could turn around and be kindness itself. Now he wanted to help his wife the only way he could, to let her know he was with her, and would be until the last.

"I love you, El," he whispered.

She smiled faintly. "And I love you, Hart. You should sleep. It might be a while yet."

"I'm not leaving you."

"No?" Her red brows climbed in her too-white face. "Good thing the bed is nice and wide."

"It's our bed."

"Yes, I know." She lightly patted the mattress. "Although I admit, I'm growing a bit tired of it at the moment."

"This will soon be over," Hart said. "And we'll snuggle down again, like an old married couple."

"Do hush. And sleep. You're cross as a bear when you don't get your sleep."

Hart softly kissed her again then laid his head on the pillow next to her.

He had no intention of sleeping, only of resting curled in her warmth, but the next thing he knew,

Eleanor was crying out again, and the midwife bustled around, a smile on her face.

"It's now, Your Grace," the midwife said. "I believe the little gentleman is coming. Time for you and his lordship to go."

Hart smoothed Eleanor's hair. "I'm not leaving."

The midwife made an impatient noise. "Your Grace . . ."

"Let him stay," Eleanor said. "If he faints, it will be his own fault. Make certain you fall out of the way on the carpet, my love."

The midwife looked unhappy, but she subsided.

Ian likewise stayed. He remained on his chair while Beth rose excitedly to help.

Hart was surprised how much Ian's silent presence comforted him. His volatile little brother, who'd needed so much help in the past, was now a rock in the roiling stream of Hart's world.

I can always find you, Ian had told him once. He'd meant that he'd know when Hart needed him, would be there, no matter what.

Eleanor screamed. She seized Hart's hand and hung on.

She crushed his fingers with amazing strength. Hart gritted his teeth, holding her steady, while her body tightened, her face beading with sweat.

The midwife and maid helped bend Eleanor's legs, settling her knees, covering her modestly. Eleanor shoved the sheets aside impatiently, her breasts straining against her dressing gown as she arched.

"Push, Your Grace," the midwife said. "Like I explained to you. Give the little fellow a shove."

Eleanor's face twisted as she obeyed, tears leaking from the corners of her eyes. Hart kissed her fingers, still tight around his. "You're strong, love," he said. "You're so strong."

Eleanor wailed in pain. She clenched Hart's hand even harder, her other fist bunching the sheets.

"He's coming, Your Grace," the midwife said. "Not much longer."

"I see him." Beth said, her smile wide. "El, I see his little head."

"Or hers," Hart said. "It might be a her."

Eleanor opened her eyes and looked at him, the blue swimming with tears. "What do you know, Hart Mackenzie? He's a . . . " She trailed off into another wail.

"He's coming," the midwife said. "Here. Quickly."

A maid was there with blankets, Beth standing with fingers steepled against her lips, the midwife frowning in concentration.

Eleanor gave one final, agonized heave, and the midwife cried out in triumph.

She bent over the blanket the maid held, and after a long, breath-stopping moment, the first shrieks—loud and angry—of a new Mackenzie rang out.

"Welcome to the world, your lordship," the midwife said.

She lifted the blanket, the baby glistening and red, still attached at his tummy to his mother. A sheaf of dark hair sprouted from his head, his tiny face screwed up, and he roared.

Hart sat up, tears blurring the wondrous sight. He touched a broad finger to his child's face.

"He's beautiful," Hart whispered. "El, he's beautiful."

Eleanor was laughing, tears spilling down her face. She reached for her baby, and the midwife gently put him into her arms.

"We'll get him all cleaned up and fed for you, Your Grace."

"In a moment," El said, her voice weak but rapt. "In a moment."

Hart kissed Eleanor's forehead and drew her close, his fingertips resting gently on his son, his hand almost as large as the lad's little body. The baby waved his fists, his cries announcing to the world that he'd arrived, and he was hungry.

Hart wanted to break down and weep; he wanted this moment to never end.

El touched the boy's cheek. "Hello, Alec." She smiled at him then slanted a sly look at Hart. "A wee little lad. I told you."

"I'll never doubt you again," Hart said. Then his tears came, and he didn't bother to stop them.

"How's the family, then?" Isabella entered the room an hour later, bringing in the family that had been kept out. Ian watched them from the sofa across the room, where he sat with Beth.

Mac came behind Isabella, then Ainsley and Cam, Eleanor's father, and Daniel, and with them the Mackenzie children. Ian rose to take Belle from Daniel's arms. He kissed his daughter, remembering every detail of his worry the night Beth had brought her into the world, and before that, when Jamie had come. Hart had just gone through the same ordeal.

Hart sat on the bed, his back against the headboard, his arm around Eleanor. The midwife had finished the rest of the birthing and washed the child, and the wet nurse had given him his first meal. Ian and Hart had been persuaded to step outside for the procedures, and once he'd walked out of the room, Hart's legs had buckled, and he'd nearly fallen to the floor.

Ian had caught him, holding his older brother upright in his arms, until Hart had regained his strength.

Darkness still prevailed outside, but bonfires broke the blackness, the villagers getting started on the Hogmanay celebrations. Inside Hart and Eleanor's bedchamber, all the lamps glowed, and the fire burned high, lighting up the scene.

"Hart Alec Graham Mackenzie," Eleanor's father, Alec Ramsay, was saying. He tickled the baby's cheek. "What a splendid name for a splendid little fellow."

They'd call him Alec in the family, Hart had said, in honor of Eleanor's father. Small Alec was now dozing in his mother's arms, breathing well, proclaimed healthy and strong by the midwife and the doctor who'd visited after the messiest bit was finished.

Hart looked as though someone had kicked him repeatedly. Exhaustion stained his face, his eyes red-rimmed, but his smile was strong and as arrogant as ever, as though he'd just done something uncommonly clever.

Ian's brothers shared Hart's pride, holding up their own children so they could greet their new cousin.

"He's very small," Jamie informed Ian. "He won't be able to ride his pony."

"He'll grow." Beth rumpled her son's hair. "In a few years, you'll be racing him."

Jamie looked doubtful. "He's even smaller than Belle."

"Not for long, I wager," Daniel said in his deep voice. "Mackenzie men grow tall." He pressed a fist to his chest and laughed down at Jamie.

Bellamy and Curry carried in trays of wine, whiskey, and champagne. Hart grabbed a glass and drank heavily, this time keeping it down.

The others raised glasses in a toast. "To the newest addition to the family," Mac said. "God help him."

"He's our First Footer," Isabella said, lifting her champagne glass. "The first into the house for the New Year."

"To the First Footer!" Mac and Daniel shouted. Glasses clinked, and champagne disappeared.

"You've lost your bet, Uncle Hart," Daniel said. "Forty guineas you owe me, I think."

"Hart, you rogue," Eleanor exclaimed. "You told me you didn't think it was proper to wager on your own child."

Hart shrugged. "I thought I had a good chance. I'll make good on my bet."

"Well, *I've* won quite a packet. Haven't I, Danny?"

"Ye have, Auntie. As have I. I always trust the mother."

"Mother." Eleanor held Alec close. "That sounds nice. And here is Papa."

She handed the baby to Hart. Hart took him, his expression softening to wonder, everything hard in him suddenly gone.

The others raised glasses once more. Ian put his arm around Beth and sank into her warmth, hefting his daughter in one arm, while his son sat happily in his mother's. This time next year, their little family would be larger, and Ian's happiness would expand yet again.

"They change you," Ian said to Hart. "We're not the same now."

"Bloody good thing," Cameron rumbled.

"Aye," Hart said. He leaned to his wife. "Thank you, El, for saving my life."

Eleanor winked at Ian as she moved to kiss Hart's lips. "You are most welcome, love."

"Do you feel you've changed that much?" Beth asked Ian much later.

The day was starting, the Hogmanay celebrations would commence soon, but Ian and Beth lay in their bedchamber, entwined and bare, the covers keeping them from the cold world.

Jamie and Belle had been taken back to the nursery for their breakfasts, both chattering about Alec and New Year's, and the unusual excitement in the house. Nanny Westlock had taken charge, and Ian had led Beth, exhausted though she wouldn't admit it, back to bed.

Ian had gathered Beth into his arms, and they'd celebrated with passionate, warm lovemaking. Ian's desire and love tangled inside him, blotting out all that was terrible and brutal in the world. Now, he trailed open-mouthed kisses down Beth's body, loving her softness.

"Ian?" Beth prompted, her voice low and sleep-filled.

Instead of answering, Ian reached into the drawer in the bedside table and pulled out the tissue-wrapped package he'd been saving to give Beth for Hogmanay. He laid it on her bare chest and pressed a kiss to her breast.

"You didn't have to get me anything," Beth exclaimed, though her face softened in pleasure. "You did so much with that wondrous surprise for Jamie."

"Open it," Ian said.

Beth undid the wrapping, which fell to the sheets, and drew a quick breath when she saw what lay inside. A locket of heavy silver rested in her hand. Beth pried open the locket, her eyes shining.

Inside were pictures, drawn and colored by Mac, of the two children, Jamie on the left, and Belle on the right. The pictures were tiny, yet Mac had executed them in fine detail.

"Ian, it's perfect."

"The locket was my mother's."

"Oh." Beth's expression went quiet. She closed the locket and held it close. "Then I'll treasure it all the more."

Ian had very little from his mother, but he'd always kept the locket safe. But Beth should have it. His mother would have liked that.

Beth laid it and the wrappings carefully on the bedside table. "Thank you, Ian."

"Mmm." Ian lowered his head back to her breast, licked around her satin areola, and drew it into his mouth.

"You didn't answer before," Beth said, her voice

going soft. "Do you feel you've changed? Being a husband and a father?"

Of course he had. She knew that—why did she need to ask? "It's better now," Ian said. He licked her nipple until it stood up in a fine point. "Much better."

"I'm inclined to agree with you."

Ian's thoughts went back to the funeral they'd attended the day Beth had broken the bowl. Death, sorrow, the loss of something he treasured. Instead of sinking into darkness and despair, Ian had walked forward, moving to what had been important—Beth, Jamie, Belle.

Beth had let him do that. He'd never have been able to sort out his thoughts or focus on what was vital in his life without her.

"Much better," Ian repeated. He kissed between her breasts and moved to her lips, sliding over her body to enter her again. "Thank you, my Beth," he said, echoing Hart's words to Eleanor.

Beth's beautiful smile spread over her face as Ian looked straight into her eyes. "You're welcome, Ian Mackenzie."

A NOTE FROM THE AUTHOR

*J*hope you've enjoyed *A Mackenzie Family Christmas: The Perfect Gift!* I decided to write this short book to give readers a glimpse of the Mackenzies' lives after events in *The Duke's Perfect Wife.* I thought it would be fun to write about all the couples, plus such characters as Lloyd Fellows, rather than focus on one romance, so that readers could enjoy a visit with their favorite Mackenzies.

A Bit about the Series

I have deep love for the Mackenzies series, which began with *The Madness of Lord Ian Mackenzie.* The Mackenzie brothers—Ian, Mac, Cameron, Hart, and Cam's son, Daniel, walked into my head one day and wouldn't leave me alone. I could think of nothing but the Mackenzie men, morning, noon, and night. I was compelled to write the books, even though I hadn't actually sold them to my publisher—I slipped *Madness of Lord*

Ian into my last contract at Dorchester, which had simply said "novel-length historical romance."

Madness released to great critical success, but then things that writers dread started to happen. My publisher was on its way to bankruptcy. They talked of not publishing *Lady Isabella's Scandalous Marriage* until 18 months after Ian's release, and soon stopped shipping printed books at all. I knew if the series was going to continue, I had to go elsewhere.

I was fortunate that my editor at Berkley was interested in the series, which is highly unusual. Most publishers want to publish brand new series from book one so they can develop the series as they like. I was lucky — people were talking about me abandoning the Mackenzies and starting something new. But then Berkley bought reprint rights to *Madness of Lord Ian* and my paranormal romance, *Pride Mates*, I signed contracts for the next books, and we went on from there.

And here we are.

To be kept informed about what's coming up in this series, please join my newsletter here:

http://eepurl.com/47kLL

Also check my website:

https://www.jenniferashley.com

where I post updates when I have them.

Thank you, and my very best wishes,

Jennifer Ashley

MACKENZIE FAMILY TREE

Ferdinand Daniel Mackenzie (Old Dan) 1330-1395
First Duke of Kilmorgan
= m. Lady Margaret Duncannon
|
Fourteen generations
|
Daniel William Mackenzie 1685-1746(?)
(9th Duke of Kilmorgan)
= m. Allison MacNab
|
6 sons
Daniel Duncannon Mackenzie (1710-1746)

William Ferdinand Mackenzie (1714-1746?)
=m. **Josette Oswald**
|
Glenna Oswald (stepdaughter)
Duncan Ian Mackenzie (1748-1836)
Gowan William Mackenzie (1750-1838)

Magnus Ian Mackenzie (1715-1734)

Angus William Mackenzie (1716-1746)

Alec William Ian Mackenzie (1716-1746?)

=m. Genevieve Millar (d. 1746)

|

Jenny (Genevieve Allison Mary) Mackenzie
(1746-1837)

=m2. **Lady Celia Fotheringhay**

|

Magnus Edward Mackenzie (1747-1835)

Malcolm Daniel Mackenzie (1720-1802)
(10th Duke of Kilmorgan from 1746)

= m. **Lady Mary Lennox**

|

Angus Roland Mackenzie 1747-1822
(11th Duke of Kilmorgan)
= m. Donnag Fleming

|

William Ian Mackenzie (The Rake) 1780-1850
(12th Duke of Kilmorgan)
= m. Lady Elizabeth Ross

|

Daniel Mackenzie, 13th Duke of Kilmorgan (1824-1874)
(1st Duke of Kilmorgan, English from 1855)
= m. Elspeth Cameron (d. 1864)

|

Hart Mackenzie (b. 1844)
14th Duke of Kilmorgan from 1874

(2nd Duke of Kilmorgan, English)
= m1. Lady Sarah Graham (d. 1876)
|
(Hart Graham Mackenzie, d. 1876)

= m2. **Lady Eleanor Ramsay**
|
Hart Alec Graham Mackenzie (b. 1885)
Malcolm Ian Mackenzie (b. 1887)

Cameron Mackenzie
= m1. Lady Elizabeth Cavendish (d. 1866)
|
Daniel Mackenzie = m. **Violet Devereaux**

Cameron Mackenzie = m2. **Ainsley Douglas**
|
Gavina Mackenzie (b. 1883)
Stuart Mackenzie (b. 1885)

"Mac" (Roland Ferdinand) Mackenzie
= m. **Lady Isabella Scranton**
|
Aimee Mackenzie (b. 1879, adopted 1881)
Eileen Mackenzie (b. 1882)
Robert Mackenzie (b. 1883)

Ian Mackenzie = m. **Beth Ackerley**
|
Jamie Mackenzie (b. 1882)
Isabella Elizabeth Mackenzie (Belle) (b. 1883)
Megan Mackenzie (b. 1885)

Lloyd Fellows = m. **Lady Louisa Scranton**

|

Elizabeth Fellows (b. 1886)
William Fellows (b. 1888)
Matthew Fellows (b. 1889)

McBride Family

Patrick McBride = m. Rona McDougal
Sinclair McBride = m.1 Margaret Davies (d. 1878)

|

Caitriona (b. 1875)
Andrew (b. 1877)

m.2 **Roberta "Bertie" Frasier**

Elliot McBride = m. **Juliana St. John**

Ainsley McBride = m.1 John Douglas (d. 1879)

|

Gavina Douglas (d.)

= m.2 **Lord Cameron Mackenzie**

|

Gavina Mackenzie (b. 1883)
Stuart Mackenzie (b. 1885)

Steven McBride (Captain, Army)
= m. **Rose Barclay**
(Dowager Duchess of Southdown)

Note: Names in **bold** indicate main characters in the
Mackenzie series

Historical Mysteries

Kat Holloway "Below Stairs" Victorian Mysteries

(writing as Jennifer Ashley)

A Soupçon of Poison

Death Below Stairs

Scandal Above Stairs

Death in Kew Gardens

Captain Lacey Regency Mystery Series

(writing as Ashley Gardner)

The Hanover Square Affair

A Regimental Murder

The Glass House

The Sudbury School Murders

The Necklace Affair

A Body in Berkeley Square

A Covent Garden Mystery

A Death in Norfolk

A Disappearance in Drury Lane

Murder in Grosvenor Square

The Thames River Murders

The Alexandria Affair

A Mystery at Carlton House

Murder in St. Giles

Death at Brighton Pavilion

The Gentleman's Walking Stick

(short stories: in print in

The Necklace Affair and Other Stories)

Leonidas the Gladiator Mysteries

(writing as Ashley Gardner)

Blood Debts

(More to come)

Mystery Anthologies

Murder Most Historical

Past Crimes

Riding Hard

(Contemporary Romance)

Adam

Grant

Carter

Tyler

Ross

Kyle

Ray

Snowbound in Starlight Bend

Nvengaria Series

(paranormal historical)

Penelope & Prince Charming

The Mad, Bad Duke

Highlander Ever After

The Longest Night

Regency Pirate Series

The Pirate Next Door

The Pirate Hunter

The Care and Feeding of Pirates

ABOUT THE AUTHOR

New York Times bestselling and award-winning author Jennifer Ashley has written more than 85 published novels and novellas in romance, urban fantasy, and mystery under the names Jennifer Ashley, Allyson James, and Ashley Gardner. Her books have been nominated for and won Romance Writers of America's RITA (given for the best romance novels and novellas of the year), several *RT BookReviews* Reviewers Choice awards (including Best Urban Fantasy, Best Historical Mystery, and Career Achievement in Historical Romance), and Prism awards for her paranormal romances. Jennifer's books have been translated into more than a dozen languages and have earned starred reviews in *Publisher's Weekly* and *Booklist*.

More about Jennifer's series can be found at http://www.jenniferashley.com.

CPSIA information can be obtained
at www.ICGtesting.com
Printed in the USA
BVHW071945110219
539954BV00012B/1410/P

9 781946 455413